TERRA GAIA

UTOPIA FOR HUMANKIND

ERIC WILKINS

ISBN:
978-1-966235-16-3 (paperback)
978-1-966235-17-0 (hardback)
978-1-966235-18-7 (ebook)

Published by:

OMNIBOOK Co.
99 Wall Street, Suite 118
New York, NY 10005 USA
+1-866-216-9965
www.omnibook.org

For e-book purchase: Kindle on Amazon, Barnes and Noble
Book purchase: Amazon.com, Barnes & Noble, and
www.omnibook.org

Omnibook titles may be purchased in bulk for educational,
business, fund-raising, or sales promotional use. For more
information please e-mail admin@omnibook.org

CONTENTS

Those whom read this chronicle of my future diary sent back in time should not in your life span be afraid. However to be totally realistic, future facts certainly are appropriate for you to become aware of the concealed circumstance that earthlings in your future will soon realize that a mysterious dark anomaly is traveling towards humanities own planet Earth.

Humans ultimately realize that humankind will have no ability to deal with the fearful approach of the Creator's Monster Nemesis that is destined to arrive at humanities own solar system in your not to distance future.

Let me assure you that Earth's encounter with a black hole is an ordeal that you shouldn't fear in your time-span. However, a few generations past your existence, future earthlings will not be exempt from the drastic events that will ultimately happen.

The ARC project that was assembled by the United States Government in my year of 3022 represented a select group of 169 humans that would fight with all of our abilities to somehow survive the encounter with this approaching dark nemesis that is vectored towards our own planetary system. It's uniquely inevitable that a few lucky survivors will enter a new dimension like no human could possibly imagine.

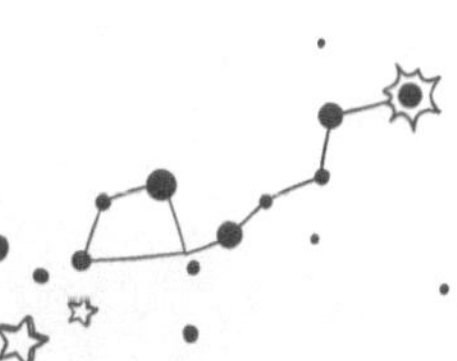

CHAPTER 1

AWARENESS BEGINS

POSSIBLY FROM YOUR timeline of a quarter of a century past the year 2000 or so, it's not so important to your well being at the moment. The facts remain that from my time period of 3022, Earth dwellers and many scientist of the world had come to the conclusion that Earth's eminent destruction would occur in our not too distant future.

Astronomers around the globe had soon identified and confirmed the massive dark nemesis predicted to enter the solar system. Panic fear and much more corruption began among the populace from humans that dreaded and feared the idea of extinction. A dark destroyer of all matter was approaching and humans had no other option other than to except the reality of Earth's own pending demise.

Examine the possibly that the reader's point of view could never be aware of such a devastating end to the world. There is no way any human of your time could possibly know that trillions of biological species that had evolved into existence for four and a half billion years would not exist anymore. I attempted to somehow inject a message back in a time capsule in hopes that a warning could possibly be relayed to present day humans.

Nine hundred and ninety-eight years in your future, the black hole's approach towards this solar system will be first detected.

CHAPTER 2

DISCOVERER OF DOOM

It's September 14th in my future year of 3022.

I Galena Dresden began my shift that Friday night at the Keck Hawaiian Observatory around 8:15 pm.

Keck Observatory had survived for over a thousand years but had been updated tremendously compared to its original version consisting of 36 hexagonal thirty feet diameter mirrors that worked in unisom to form a single huge reflection mirror.

In the future version of the Keck telescope, it had increased in size by adding 180 more ten-meter mirrors. That update had increased its parabolic reflection capability by 850 percent from the original construction capacity.

Future technology had allowed the Keck telescope to be directly linked with the updated version of the JWST-3 telescope that is stationed at a specific Lagrange point between the earth and the moon's cislunar balanced gravity well.

My study directive on this Friday night shift was to instruct the telescope towards an almost empty sector of space called the Bootes Void or as some astronomers referred to as the Great Dark Nothing.

CHAPTER 3

THE GREAT DARK NOTHING OF THE BOOTES VOID

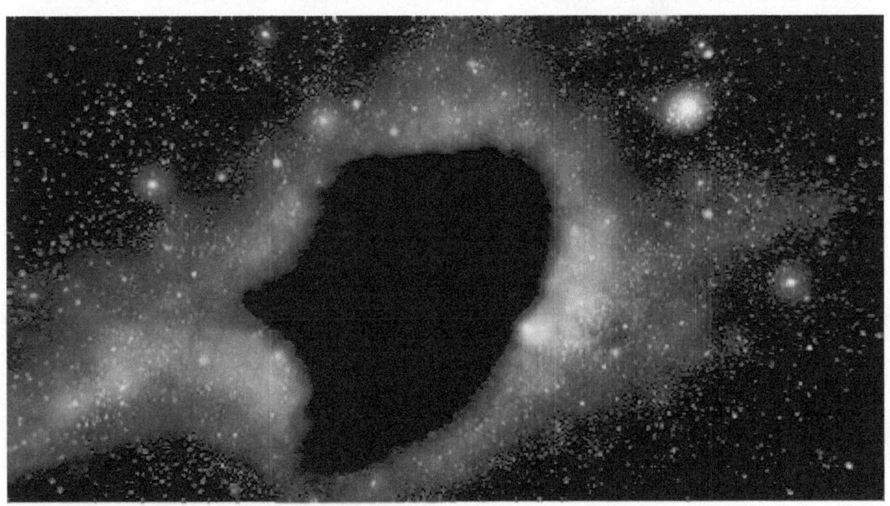

THE BOÖTES VOID is sometimes referred to as the great dark nothing consisting of an approximate spherical region of space found in the vicinity of the constellation Bootes containing very few galaxies hence its name The Great Nothing.

This huge dark region of space has a radius of 62 mega parsecs or nearly 330 million light-years.

The Bootes void's diameter is 124 mega parsecs or 660 million light-years across. This ominous dark area is one of the largest known voids in the universe and is referred to as one of several very scarce super voids.

The Great Nothing was first discovered in the year 1981 by Robert Kirshner as part of a survey of galactic red shifts. The center of the great void is located 700 million light-years from Earth at approximate right assertion, 14h 50m and declamation 46°. The Hercules Super cluster forms part of the near edge of the void.

After about 20 minutes I had managed to program the input codes to begin focusing the telescope towards the center of the Bootes Void. Electric motors engaged as the telescope began focusing all 216 mirrors each following a specific movement sequence.

Several more minutes passed while all mirrors rotated and locked into position towards the directed co ordinance revealing a single gigantic reflection of total blackness. The Bootes Void projected its glorified mysterious image of deep-dark mysterious non-light across the labs giant video screen.

It had been thirty minutes since I'd returned from my mid-shift break when an alarm diverted my attention to a tiny pinprick of darker than darkness that now appeared on the telescopic screen.

My first response was that it must be a glitch in the computer software that could possibly prove that the anomaly's existence really wasn't there at all. I was mesmerized and couldn't stop staring at the tinniest pinpoint of purple-black radiation that I had ever experienced in my 37-year lifespan.

The Bootes Void itself was very dark black in color but this pinprick of darkness stood out and was way darker than anything past the ultraviolet scale of the spectrum. I sat mesmerized for nearly an hour hypnotized by the radiating black pinprick of non-light that I had ever experienced.

I surmised and speculated of my own knowledge that the center of the Great Nothing was well over seven hundred million light years distance from Earth.

With computer assistance using a parallax of the Earth Moon system, I was able to zero in on the blackness of the darker than dark pinpoint. I had the computer run analysis several times and I soon realized the extreme seriousness of this discovery.

Scarce details as of yet but parallax calculations of computer scans revealed that this pinprick of darkness coming out of the Bootes Void could possible be as close as a parsec away or to be more specific, 3.26 light years from our own solar system. As far as the pinprick's speed and direction, subsequent studies would reveal vital facts and answers under further expert analysis. That's when the real concern begins.

CHAPTER 4

REPORTING MY DISCOVERY

AFTER A LONG exciting shift around 8:15 AM, I preceded straight to the headquarters of Matthew Sagan the head astronomy professor at Keck University.

I was totally possessed with urgent intent to inform Professor Sagan of my discovery during my shift the night before.

Normally after a shift I would be heading to my home approximately sixteen kilometers away from the facility. I sat nervously outside his office urgently awaiting the Professor's attention. I realized that if my discovery is confirmed by other astronomers that It could possible be a planet-changing event.

Professor Sagan showed up around 10:30 and soon we sat comfortably conversing my new discovery details in his office. Professor Sagan insisted that I call him by his first name Matthew and after several minutes of study of my unique details, he also became very excited about this fascinating discovery.

After the meeting he soon informed the world astronomy association of my new discovery for further analysis. Before ending the meeting we scheduled future weekly meetings to become updated on other astronomers results.

I understood that it would take time for others to verify my discovery. With the help of other astronomers in future days we should be able to determine the exact size distance direction and speed of the pinprick of blackness that I Galena Dresden discovered that morning that was excreting out of the Booted Void.

It was approximately 4:30 AM that Saturday morning when I first spotted a strange anomaly in the center of the Bootes Void. I strained visually to see the details but a fuzzy darkness obscured the edges of what I was not sure of what I was visually seeing.

A faint darker distinction of the fuzzy pinpricks edge revealed something was there but it was visually hard to identify the pinprick that was even darker than the slight lighter fuzz surrounding the anomaly. Total magnification first estimated from the parallax that this dark mass was approximately a parsec away from this solar system.

CHAPTER 5

POPULACE PANIC

Major Governments of Earth had tried desperately to keep the new discovery secrete but it wasn't long before this ominous fact began leaking and circulating through the news media of planet Earth. At first there wasn't much public concern but months after the discovery it was confirmed that the dark speck from the Bootes Void was definitely moving at a speed and direction that would ultimately encounter this solar system and devour all the planets moons and matter contained.

That's when the real populace panic began.

The immediate days news after this unique discovery had many institutions focusing in on the pinprick black fuzzy darker than darkness image shooting out of the Bootes Void.

For weeks many astronomy scientific scholars of Earth intensely investigated the strange anomaly and many speculated and postulated their opinions of what it could mean for humanity. Government officials around the globe began intensive studies of the new discovery of Galena Dresden.

Three weeks passed my discovery results revealed detailed analysis of the black object. This threatening pinpoint of darkness was indeed moving towards our solar system at an estimated speed of 93,000 miles per. second or in other words half the speed of light in the cold vacuum of space.

Many scientists soon concluded from these detailed facts that in 2,555 days or seven years, if the direction and speed of the anomaly

13

remained the same, planet earth and this entire solar system was ultimately doomed. In seven years the black nemesis would begin destroying the outer edge of this solar system.

It was now October 8th, 3023 and worldwide panic was beginning to occur around the globe. The eighteen billion people of Earth soon knew the news of this approaching doom.

No officials anywhere knew what to expect or what to do. Later further analysis of the anomaly revealed that the pinprick of darkness was estimated to be twice as large as the solar system's diameter.

October the 10th 3023, a special security meeting was initiated at 10 AM at the United Nation's Committee of National Disaster to discuss the known facts and potential threat of the newly discovered object that recently was discovered coming out of the blackness of the Bootes Void.

It was the darkness of the Bootes Void itself that enabled this pinprick anomaly to be concealed for so long in the deep blackness until it got close enough to be detected when it was only a parsec distance from Earth.

A Parsec is a unit of astronomical length based on the distance from Earth at which stellar parallax is one second of arc and equal to 3.258 light-years distance.

Postulated by mathematicians that configured the speed of the anomaly, it was estimated that the matter-gobbling monster of darkness would reach the edge of our solar system in 2,515 days or slightly less than seven years.

By day 2,489-bn, the entire world's chaos caused suicides, murder and crime that increased dayly. Fires burned in many nations around the planet while food supplies dwindled to alarming necessities for billion of humans that daily struggled with the consequences of all human life ending forever.

I myself tried to focus my specific attention during my subsequent shift observations on attempting to verify the pinpricks exact speed and direction.

I discovered that night that most scientific calculations confirmed that the anomaly was indeed headed for our solar system. I finished my shift on day 2487 and retired to my residence with a heavy heart and deep since of dread for all humankind.

Reaching home, I showered and attempted to sleep but the seriousness of the situation always invaded my thoughts and prevented me from any constructive sleep.

My thoughts kept straying to my own personal existence and accomplishments so far in life. Here I was a 37-year-old female astronomer who had been the first to discover the approaching doom. My sense of dread for discovering the approaching end of it all was always subconsciously deeply blaming myself for showing up for work that night of Sep the 14th.

Yes I was aware that had I not been the first to discover the black threat many other astronomers on Earth would have discovered it sooner or later. Still, I blamed myself for being the first. Of the six hours I tossed and turned, no helpful rest was obtained by my struggled attempt.

CHAPTER 6

ONE OF ONE-SIXTY-NINE

IT WAS DAY 2196 and almost a year after first discovery when I was startled awake around 1:30 pm by an intense banging on my apartment door. Startled awake as I was, I struggled to manage putting on my robe and sleepily stumbled my way from my bedroom through the hall and opened my door with the safety chain still attached allowing 5 inches of outside view.

I was indeed surprised to see a brigade of six full dressed military officers standing on my small front shaded stoup. Clutching my robe tighter I unhooked the chain and opened the door all the way.

The head official was an oriental slim officer and spoke with a firm voice while introducing himself as Admiral Nelson Tyson from the Pentagon's National Defense Department. Behind the Admiral stood five more naval officers dressed in full uniform. In wonderment of the present circumstance, I invited them in to inquire what this was all about.

Admiral Tyson informed me that he worked directly for the Pentagon and answers directly to the commander in chief President Jessica Rogers.

The Presidents orders was to immediately come here and instruct me to gather my necessities and report to the Whitehouse for a security briefing with the USA president on the present status of the Bootes Void anomaly.

It took me about forty-five minutes to gather my necessities before I was quickly ushered out of the door to a waiting long black limousine that ultimately delivered me to an official military helicopter at Honolulu International Airport.

Terra Gaia

that ultimately delivered me to an official military helicopter at Honolulu International Airport.

CHAPTER 7

PRESIDENTIAL MEETING

By nine-thirty that night I waited patiently in the Oval office escorted by two security guards that had hardly spoken except to usher me into a room instructing me to sit and wait for the president to appear.

I stood alert as President Jessica Rogers entered the room where I waited with the two security guards. The president quickly dismissed the guards and instructed me to relax and have a seat in a soft chair directly in front of her.

President Rogers was dressed in today's progressive attire and stood out as a very intriguing female figure. Approximately 50 years of age she still had her youthful beauty but the entirety of her stressful job had certainly begun to show signs of aging beyond her years.

She looked at me for several seconds with a worried expression before she spoke in an absolute total top-secret whispered tone.

This is total top secret. As of tomorrow, this government has 2195 days to attempt a mission for a group of humans to possibly survive the coming apocalypse. She proceeded to secretly place in my hands a list of 169 names that were chosen to report immediately to Cheyenne Mountain Operation Center in Colorado.

My name Galena Dresden was listed on line 162 of the document that she provided.

President Rogers knew the facts of the approaching dark-nemesis and began revealing the plan for 169 individuals to shelter underground in hopes of somehow allowing a few humans to survive in a worst-case scenario. It's all we have she stated.

President Rogers secretly informed me that she couldn't provide many details on the project but that I would be fully informed once I arrive at the underground base under Cheyenne Mountain.

She informed me that I had been chosen due to my astronomy science achievements and adamantly expressed that my knowledge was very much needed and appreciated on this secret project entitled ARC which is an acronym for Apocalypse–Resistance-Colony.

President Jessica Rogers finalized our meeting informing me that the secret project's name should not be revealed to anyone and specifics of the ARC details would be revealed when I arrived at Cheyenne base in Colorado.

She subsequently thanked me for my time but before she dismissed me, she asked if I had any questions but stated emphatically that she was limited on revealing facts on the ARC secret project.

Without hesitation I accepted her proposal and thanked her for including me in this secret attempt to somehow to survive.

By 11 AM that next morning on day 2193, I was one of six other passengers strapped in as the military helicopter flew across the Pacific Ocean. Four hours after mid-air refueling over California we began approaching our destination. The military copter hovered for sixty-seconds before gently settling down just outside the main entrance of Cheyenne Mountain Base.

Several of us aboard already knew each other but not much conversing about ARC occurred during the flight. I supposed that they must be under the same gag order that I was sworn to.

Seven of us departed the craft steeping to the concrete below the slow swirling winds of the copter's blades. We were immediately ushered by four armed guards towards a giant steel doorway a hundred yards uphill from where the helicopter had landed.

I was the fourth person in line as we topped a hill and entered through a humongous Iron Gate doorway. My mind couldn't help but wonder what this secret project was all about and how could anyone possibly survive an apocalyptic nemesis vacuum cleaner that was twice as large as the solar system?

CHAPTER 8

ARC OR APOCALYPSE RESISTANCE COLONY

We were escorted to an underground conference room where Major Nicholas Griffin greeted the seven of us. The Major silently gestered our group of three women and four men towards another nearby room that was identified with dull-lit letters spelling out Initiation Room over the door.

As we were allowed in we each sat in separate chairs in a semicircle arrangement. Major Griffin closed and locked the door and proceeded to a slightly raised podium in front of our seven half circled chair arrangment.

Major Griffin a smooth skinned Nigerian military admiral in his 40's spoke out with distinctive military tone and began his first words of encouragement.

Apocalypse Resistance Colony or ARC, is the name and ultimate intention of this proposed project. This facility underground at Cheyenne Base is being totally revamped in an attempt to shelter the 169 names included on the Presidential preferred list. ARC will be an unlimited budget funded project for a grandiose attempt for 169 humans to survive this approaching nemesis monster.

I totally understand that such a grand undertaking seems like an impossible task to perform without fully knowing the facts you are about to learn.

We are so thankful for a new scientific discovery by our next speaker Professor Joshua Jarvis that I will introduce shortly.

It has been ordered by the president that this project is an all out investment attempt for the possibility of a select few humans surviving.

Because of Professor Jarvis's recent new discovery it just might be possible for the ARC colony to somehow survive when the nemesis swallows the solar system.

Major Griffin then pressed a buzzer that allowed the door to electronically unlock.

To my unexpected surprise, into the room steps the most handsome Jesus figure of a man that I ever dreamed possible.

I had no intentions of romance during this dangerous mission but I couldn't help but notice that the other two women seemed just as impressed as I was at the handsome figure that now stepped to the podium where Major Griffin stood waiting.

Joshua Jarvis had long silver white streaked hair and an athletic build that many women would love to see in any man. Even the men seem to envy this unusual physic of this person named Joshua Jarvis. I can't explain it but it was almost like his presence had a glow about him as he stepped behind the podium.

I certainly wasn't here for romance but being a normal biological woman, I was immediately impressed by his masculine presence even before he stepped up to the podium to introduce himself.

His neatly trimmed facial features and long soft flowing silver-white streaked hair had indeed intrigued my silent personal thoughts. He paused a few moments before beginning to speak. His soothing voice had a tone that immediately focused the listener's attention.

CHAPTER 9
PROFESSOR JOSHUA JARVIS

Hello everyone, I'm Professor Joshua Jarvis. I am the head chemistry professor from Cornell University. I suppose that's the reason some of my students refer to me as Doctor JJ as my nickname.

I'm 33 years old and for the past 10 years I have devoted my research and study on how to manipulate matter chemically. Due to a recent discovery of mine and two of my students, the government has instructed me to participate in this most important ARC Project that's ever been conceived in humanities history.

Our most recent discovery in atomic chemistry is what this ARC program will use to attempt to build a new structure that surrounds the outside of this entire underground base.

This mixture of certain properties will be poured like concrete and will resist any extreme pressure and heat and cause it to dissipate around the new outside of this coated base.

Recently, my colleagues and myself have discovered a chemical bonding process of how to mix atomic black ions with hardening acrylic polymers to form a hot liquid substance that will super harden when poured and cooled around a formed structure such as this ARC underground base.

Abirm is an acronym for Atomic Black Ion Resistance Mixture. We have already began mass production of Abirm at a close by former vacant facility located twenty-kilometers from this base.

At this very moment, crews are already in the process of removing all matter around this underground structure to a height of a little over three meters or ten feet. Under the floors will be formed up and excavated first.

Once all the matter is cleared above below and around this base, pipes will be inserted extending upwards to allow the Abirm mixture to pour so it will settle then cool and get extremely hard. Once the lower base is completely poured, we will then begin coating the remaining surrounding walls and once completely finished, the entire base will have a three-meter thick Abirm protection coating.

As of sunrise tomorrow on day 2192, it is estimated that it will take approximately 1224 days to remove all the matter completely around ten-feet above and below this already 9,000 feet underground mountain base.

Once all goes well with the structural forming and feeder pipe installation, it will take approximately 968 more days to get this large amount of Abirm mixture created and poured.

It is estimated that we should accomplish the multi-trillion-gallon Abirm pour in 609 days. That will allow the Abirm pour to be completed almost a year before the apocalypse arrives at the edge of our doomed solar system.

I'll proceed by explaining a little more about Abirm's unique properties. By melting magnetized nuclear waste, we grind up and mix disposable uranium 238 with molten super black ion acrylic polymers. After an intense magnification process, this unique process results in creation of magnetic molten Abirm.

Under extreme hydraulically compressed pressure, the mixture remains molten and is the consistency of thick concrete.

The Abirm plant at the base of the mountain will be running up to full capacity in thirty-days and once that occurs, we should be able to produce a truckload of Abirm per. hour.

As each load is created, it will remain molten for about four hours before it starts the cooling process and begins its hardening phase.

That four-hour period will allow ample time for each load to be dispatched here and be continuously fed its mixture directly into the feeder tubes.

Transport drivers of all Abirm delivery trucks will be required to wear hazardous material clothing as a precautionary safety measure. Yes Abirm is radioactive but once pored around the base, the hardened surrounding circumference of Abirm will protect inhabits from any harmful levels of radiation.

Joshua paused in his informative explanation to ask the seven of us if we had any questions so far.

Nervously I stood to be the first to submit a query. I tried to hide my infatuation with Joshua by ignoring his mesmerizing eyes. I was unsuccessful. I realized that I was somewhat hampered by refusing to make eye contact. Eventually as I began speaking our eyes met. I struggled with infatuation as my question was meekly posed. I asked.

I do understand your basic hypothesis but how can anyone be certain that Abirm will protect the base from such a devastating apocalyptic event?

Joshua's handsome smile relaxed momentarily but quickly issued a response.

The absolute truth is, no one knows he responded. But Joshua quickly injected, under the analysis of Abirm's properties in lavatory testing procedures, once each load of Abirm is poured and cools, it has a resistant crushing affect of super hardness that is considerably harder than diamonds.

The real truth is, Arc is the only chance to possibly survive. No one could possibly know really what will happen under extreme pressure and duress.

All that we do know is that Abirm is the hardest substance that we can create with our present technology. Abirm and the ARC project is our only option that we have for anyone inside the base to possibly survive the approaching apocalyptic Monster Nemesis.

A gentleman to my right named Raymond Taylor first introduced himself then asked Joshua what he thought the percentage of survival would be once devoured by the black hole.

There are absolutely no guarantees of survival at all. Joshua replied. No one can possible pretend to know what the actual physics inside the black hole will be like?

Even if we do somehow possibly survive, there is no possibility at this time of issuing a percentage of survivability. We are simply facing the darkest of unknowns ever postulated upon humans.

I'm assured of this indisputable fact Joshua stated in reply. Once the ARC Team focuses our attention to defeating this enigma, a focused pathway is our best and only possible option to survive this doomsday scenario.

Joshua apologized for his urgent necessary departure by saying that he had to go directly to his lavatory to initiate immediate protocols of the ARC Project. The introduction ended by instructing us that each ARC member will be put to work in their best abilities and daily briefings will be issued to all on the status of ARC project.

Joshua finished his briefing and wished us all a good day as he left the podium and exited the room.

CHAPTER 10

MY UNCONTROLLABLE INFATUATION

I TRIED NOT to follow his exit but the female instinct in me wasn't able to resist the most handsome man that I have ever seen. I instantly couldn't help but wonder if I would see him again soon. I was unwillingly hypnotized that day. It was if I had no control.

In a few years the end of the world was coming. Here I am suddenly hypnotized at first sight of a handsome man named Joshua Jarvis that I didn't even know existed 24 hours ago. The other two women in the group seemed just as impressed by his looks and outstanding personality as I was.

My personal feelings were totally out of control. Never before in all my years had I ever been so attracted to a man like Joshua Jarvis. I had just met this man tonight. I had no words to explain my feelings of infatuation. I only knew the facts of what just occurred. My controls over those feelings were unobtainable at this moment.

From the very first time that I'd laid eyes on him, I couldn't erase the picture vision in my mind of the most handsome man that I'd ever dreamed possible.

The meeting was soon adjourned and in the early morning hours of day 2192, we each were ultimately issued temporary quarters inside the base. We were indeed all exhausted at this point.

Cheyenne Base consisted of a two and a half-mile or 4.02 kilometer long tunnel straight down the center. A half-kilometer inside the tunnel you come to cross-section A. The left tunnel and the right tunnel in A Block each consisted of 20 personal living facilities. Rooms are numbered counting from the far left corridor from numbers 1 to 40 with 40 ending at the far right tunnels end on each cross block.

There are four more cross sections deeper in the tunnel labeled B through E and each cross block with the exception of E is identically numbered in the same order as block A.

A half-kilometer further in past A block is cross block B where both left and right corridors were numbered exactly the same way as A-block. Another half-kilometer in, you cross block C, and then another half kilometer to cross block D.

Two kilometers past D block you arrive at cross block E that is the deepest part of Cheyenne Base that exists under 9,570 feet of dirt above Cheyenne Mountain Base.

The left side of cross block E corridor is where grocery storage facilities and small shops are located. The right side of block E will be limited to Presidential chosen staff of 13 people including the President and Vice Presidential team.

Along the two-kilometers of tunnel past D block that leads to Block E, there were many equipment and machine storage facilities off set into the walls along the way on both sides.

After the early morning orientation of the base, the seven of us were each issued our own personal quarters. We were all issued quarters in A Block and my designated quarters was A-7.

Soon separated from the 6 others, I found myself exhaustingly heading down the left corridor of block A, I eventually found my way to the front door of room A-7. I certainly had no idea of what the accommodations were like until I inserted the pass card that I was issued.

Oval doors split and swished open from the center disappearing into the walls revealing a meter wide entrance that exposed the small accommodations of a twelve square meter military style living quarters.

Drab gray acrylic walls surrounded the entire living quarters. A small cooking area and a corner computer area and queen size bedding was mostly the entire content. In one corner a curtain-concealed a shower and commode to the right of the door when entering from the outside.

I was informed that our present clothing would be destroyed and proper clothing would be issued after we had rested and reported in to the main headquarters. We had been instructed to shed all of our clothes and insert them into the trash disposal door next to the bathroom facilities.

I was indeed exhausted. As gravity slid the rest of my clothing to the floor, I stepped silently into the warm misty soothing water spray.

Trickling warm waters and electric soft massagers allowed me to soap my entire body and after a few moments of relaxing in the steamy water, I began uncontrollably fantasizing about Joshua Jarvis. It was out of my control.

I imagined his naked body in the shower with me. My hands began massaging my breast with soapy warm water. My inner passion was rising to a point that I couldn't resist my right hand slowly lowering to my private area.

Long-minutes passed as fingered massaging began while my sexual imagination ran wild to a point of a shocking explosive orgasm more intense than I'd ever experienced.

Legs weakened from orgasmic shock, I found myself curled up in the corner of the shower floor in a dazed dream of total exhausted satisfaction. Soft water splashed all around me as I struggled to prevent falling asleep from today's adventures.

Somehow, I sleepily managed to turn the water off and drag myself up from the floor while attempting to dry my naked body. All of my sexual body areas still tingled from the experience that I had just had in the shower. I felt no quilt of my recent erotic thoughts and actions. Only total contentment was my sleepy end result that night.

The last memory of that night 2192 was of my stumbling naked dive towards the bedding provided and once 15 seconds had passed, I found myself in another satisfied dream state. I slept so sound for the first time in many earth revolutions.

CHAPTER 11

2192 DAYS BEFORE NEMESIS

Awakened around 9 AM I answered the intercom to be informed that specific clothing uniforms were delivered outside my door and that this clothing was required to be worn while inside the base.

Still naked from my eight-hour slumber I opened the door to reveal a paper-coated parcel wrapped in military fashion with a small top emblem of 56 stars on the USA flag.

Carefully unsealing the package revealed a navy-blue knee high-skirted paper uniform. On top was an envelope that contained my instructions and work order details.

I was ordered to report to the astronomy lab in Block E 41 at 8 AM on day 2190. I would be in charge of monitoring the approaching apocalyptic nemesis. I was allowed a day and a half to familiarize myself with the base operation and explore the shops to the left corridor of Block E. My astronomy lab's number E-41 was an extra-added room that existed at the very end of the tunnel of the right side tunnel of Block E.

On the very top of Cheyenne Mountain was a single 10-meter mirrored telescope that was wi-fi'd directly into the astronomy room computers. The telescope was not as strong as the Keck telescope but it was sufficient enough to zero in on the black hole as it became more detectable by the day. It would be my job to report daily about the status of the black hole's progress.

CHAPTER 12

EXPLORING THE BASE

I STILL HAD a day and a half left before reporting to my assigned duties so I decided to explore the base and end up at the shops in the left corridor of Block-E.

Outside each door a small electric transport was provided for each resident of Block-A. I pressed a release button to the left of my door and the vehicle exited from a hidden panel.

As small as the electric cart was, the three-wheeled vehicle was capable of carrying two passengers and light luggage capacity. The transport's onboard computer was programmed to go to any room on any block simply by typing in the designated base destination.

I unplugged the cart from the charger and stepped aboard to begin my ride. I typed in B Block with no room number and the cart started down the corridor headed in that direction.

Top transport speed registered 20 KPH or about twice the normal walking speed of a human.

I estimated at this speed I should be at the B crossing in approximately six minutes.

I stopped momentarily at Block B crossing and examined both left and right corridors that appeared laid out exactly like A Block. All the blocks were identical in corridor layout with the exception of main block E. Whirring electrical echoes reverberated off the walls as I proceeded along my path past C block and then D block.

It took me another 45 total minutes to reach my eventual destination of block E's crossing. I had passed several vehicles along my journey traveling in the opposite direction. Now that I had arrived at E-block, I wanted to first explore the astronomy lab where I would be providing my services.

The right side corridor of block E had an electronic barrier that required special security ID before allowing passage.

I angled my transport towards the barrier and inserted my base ID pass card into the slot. Two seconds passed and the barrier slowly opened to allow me entrance.

The Presidential side of Block-E was slightly wider than the other corridors. Past the rather large main office on the left I then passed by a cafeteria room that was across from a medical facility. A quarter-kilometer pass that I approached the end of the tunnel where the astronomy lab number E-41 was labeled above a meter wide green electrically sealed door.

I parked my transport and stepped across to insert my ID in a waste high slot on the left side of entrance. There was a soothing swish as the door parted in the center and disappeared into the walls. Exposed was a ten-meter diameter round smooth floored room. Equal spaced computer stations surrounded the circumference with the center floor completely unobstructed. That's when I first met two of my colleagues that I'd be working with.

Lacy Carpenter and Jason Tyler were already involved and hard at work tracking the distant nemesis anomaly. They eagerly filled me in on the present status of the approaching black hole and confirming the estimated arrival time.

Jason Tyler a young 27-year-old male was chosen due to his excellent marks in astronomical study from the California Institute of Technology. His excited ambition was totally committed to the success of this mission. I liked Jason. I considered him to be a great asset towards our goal.

Just as important, I soon met Lacy Carpenter. Her experience was even more impressive than Jason's.

Lacy was a very pretty 25-year-old female whose personality was as sharp as her slim figure. They both wore the same blue paper garments that I did except the men's version was designed with knee high top shorts. Undergarments were not necessary due to the required daily destruction of everyone's wearing apparel.

30th century paper clothing was normal in this future time. Paper of this century was engineered with modern techniques that gave paper the properties of cloth from earlier times. Humankind had progressed past racism and societal backgrounds. Here on the base everyone was considered equal. There was no discrimination.

It's so ironic that just as humankind was struggling past a lot of humanly flaws, they now had to deal with a monster dark nemesis that they had absolutely no control over. Its path was inevitably headed towards this solar system. Doom approached and a matter of each day revolving away towards a fearful apocalyptic destruction. Possibly the few aboard this ARC project could somehow succeed.

Maybe not but it's the only chance we have. We aboard the ARC will indeed give it our all in future attempt to somehow survive the approaching deadly Nemesis.

After a few hours of collaboration I finished my introduction to the two lab assistants and left in time to stock up on grocery items on the other side of Block-E.

I crossed out of the restricted side and drove my transport past the gate towards a line of necessity stores on Block E's left corridor. I shopped the grocery isles and stored my chosen favorites in a wheeled basket while scanning each item onto my personal ID card.

CHAPTER 13

JOSHUA APPEARS

THERE WERE ONLY five center food isles in this small food chain supply store. I rounded isle one and was shocked to see Joshua Jarvis half way up isle two.

My heart began beating faster immediately. I pondered to myself, is this extreme luck or pure destiny? He hadn't noticed me yet so I stood for long moments watching him shop grocery items.

Suddenly he looked around and caught my embarrassed-self closely observing him. He wore the male version of issued protocol except that the color of his paper uniform was plant-green in color. His stark handsome profile only emphasized his tan complexion under the lighted store isle. I stood forty-feet away and already my knees were beginning to slightly shake. I just kept nervously thinking of what to do next.

From his friendly smile I realized that he'd already recognized who I was so I began casually strolling my way up isle two to where he stood waiting.

His hazel blue eyes appeared excited to see me as I approached with my buggy of necessities.

His first words from his smooth lips spoke with sincerity well hello Galena, It's so great to see you here.

Yes indeed I replied, I've been thinking a lot about your Abirm project ever since our first meeting. I really do like what I understood about project ARC. I'm excited about your plan to attempt surviving this dreadful apocalypse.

His next words surprised me. You're a very pretty woman. Since you're the head of the ARC astronomy project, perhaps we could get together tonight and discuss further project details. I've been issued quarters in section D-21. If you could stop by around 7 o'clock tonight that would be wonderful.

I quickly agreed to his meeting proposal. I tried hard to refrain from showing excitement but I don't think I succeeded very well. I did notice that he had three bottles of red wine in his cart.

We soon parted ways and the rest of my daylight hour thoughts were filled with anticipation of tonight's rendezvous with a man that I was totally infatuated with his exotic presence. I had no control over my emotions.

After I'd made my way back to A-7, I stored my groceries and relaxed with a glass of wine at my comfort station. It was 1-PM in the afternoon of day 2292. All of my thoughts of tonight's rendezvous with Joshua Jarvis excessively dwelled uncontrollably in my mind.

I switched the video screen on and watched public enragement in the streets of the six-year away apocalypse. With all that was going on, my thought's still always reverted back to Joshua Jarvis. I couldn't control it. As relaxing time passed, I suddenly realized that I'd been sitting here for over three hours. Around 4:30, I left my comfort station to begin preparation for tonight's encounter.

CHAPTER 14

UNCONTROLLABLE PASSION

Casually discarding my paper uniform garment, I stepped as nature intended under soothing warm waters that transferred its warm energy over my entire body.

I pressed a button and the door closed and gentle massage brushes departed from the walls and began rotating cleansing soap over my body. Lost in total relaxation, my passionate mind was unable to stop thinking about Joshua. My imagination soared past tingling sensations deeply inhabiting my soul's pleasurable known experience. I had again lost control.

I attempted at first to prevent my right hand from slipping downward but that resistance was in vain after several attempts. When I first touched myself uncontrollable sexual lightning buckled my knees. I collapse in total satisfaction now corner-curled under falling waters on the floor of my quarter's shower.

Hot waters kept falling over me for several minutes while I eventually was able to revive from my sexual fantasy. Never in my life had I ever fell asleep in the shower from such sexual satisfaction. I couldn't even understand it myself. I must have slept in the falling stream of water for at least another half-hour.

It was 5:10 PM when I awoke and first stood up in the shower. I pressed the air dryer button and swirling warm air evaporated the liquid

41

while my long golden-blond hair was sucked upward by vacuumed air for quick drying.

I dressed in a fresh knee-high skirted uniform of sky-blue. My makeup took me a while longer before I was satisfied of my best appearance in the mirror.

In today's society, males or females did not require undergarments. Clothing production was so advanced that daily clothing disposal became necessary against spreading virus and diseases.

CHAPTER 15

HERE I GO

My sky-blue skirt remained open to the air breezing between my legs. My upper blouse was a shade darker while my exposed neckline revealed low shoulders and bare arms. With the exception of size, all wore durable red-trimmed open-air disposable flip-flop paper shoes.

At 6:15 PM, I mounted my transport and headed towards D-21. I didn't know what to expect but I was certainly excited about the prospect of romance being involved. I couldn't help notice the air blowing up my skirt and cooling my legs as I proceeded down the likeness of a moonshine lit corridor. Tunnel lighting was specifically synchronized with outside daylight or nighttime reality.

After 20 minutes, I passed level C and my watch registered 6:39 PM.

Nervously I steered ahead not knowing what to expect from this encounter with a man I was covertly deeply infatuated with. I was so nervous. As I approached D Block, I made the hard right turn and D-21 was the first room on the right.

Parking my transport, I cautiously stepped towards his unit door. As I did, an outside light alerted my presence and within seconds the door swished open.

There he stood in green uniform smiling with way above average handsome charm. Well hello Galena. I'm so glad that you are here. Please come in and make yourself comfortable.

CHAPTER 16

NIGHT OF ECSTASY

I WALKED IN and sat on the left side of his comfort station sofa.

His friendly chatter about the project details seemed to relieve some of the nervous tensions that I was experiencing before I arrived.

He laughed and even joked a bit about the end of the world but he was deeply sincere that we somehow could possibly survive this approaching apocalypse.

His paper green clothing uniquely revealed the masculinity of his body. It was hard for me to even take my eyes off as he approached and handed me a glass of red wine. We clicked glasses and casually sat down on his comfort sofa.

I proceeded to ask him first about his childhood because I was anxious to learn the facts of if he had a wife or was in a present relationship. He casually laughed at my request and replied, No I'm not married and my scientific research has been my relationship so far in life.

Joshua Continued. I never knew my biological parents He relented. I understand that they were killed in an accidental explosion in their research lab when I was only three years of age.

Foster parents at St. Jude Hospital in a New York City raised me and I grew up at the orphanage that was financed by the government.

As a young boy in school, I was allowed access to the my biological parents research records. Those early experiences I suppose are what gave me such a keen interest in atomic chemistry. I've been so involved in my research career that I haven't devoted much time in any sort of romantic relationships.

By now my half empty glass of red wine already had me feeling way woozier than I realized. I'd only been here a half-hour and his presence was overwhelming my resistance to temptation.

Blame it on the wine if you like but before I realized through my talking hand gestures that I had casually placed my right hand on his left leg and looked into his mesmerizing blue eyes. I immediately sensed his excitement now noticing a huge budge under his paper garment. As I starred deeply into his mesmerizing eyes we both leaned forward as our lips met softly. His left hand touched my right leg sending lightning shivers all the way up my spine. We stood and embraced tightly in a long passionate first kiss.

Within a few seconds our paper clothing fell to the floor and we began touching and caressing each other with our fingers. Our compilation momentarily broke as Joshua engaged soft music then quickly turned back to our exotic touching. My wide-open eyes now glanced down at his enormous member. In my lifetime I had never realized that a man's private member could be so large.

Melodic music enveloped the room as he gently pressed me down softly upon his bed. He eyes deliciously ravaged my nakedness enjoying every second as his hardness gained more throbs of anticipation.

Soon his fingers began massaging my breast as his heart throbbing member sent shivers across my entire body. He kissed my nipples for the longest time eventually moving his head towards my open legs.

He gasped out loud when my right hand fingers clasped around his enormous thick member. I felt explosive sparks when his tongue brushed against my private area. I was so aroused that my tongue began licking his member as he mounted me in a 69 position. He jerked and moaned when I placed my lips around the head of his thick 10-inch male member.

I took half of the length in my mouth with my tongue loaded with hot saliva. I licked all the way around his thickness while listening to his moans as it moved slowly back in forth.

At first he lightly teased me when suddenly his tongue thrust deep inside me and penetrated my passion's G spot. I let out a passionate scream as my juice filled his mouth. He inserted two fingers and began moving his head in circles savoring the juices I was excreting. I was thrusting my hips upward into his gorgeous neatly trimmed bearded face. I'd already had three orgasms from his passionate tongue probing and he just kept going with determined lust.

My latest scream of passion had me grabbing his huge manhood and pushing it as deep as I could down my throat. It was so large I only managed half of his length covered with my saliva. I began thrashing my head up and down on his member licking the circumference passionately with each thrust.

Faster he began moving until suddenly he screamed with delight as he excreted a stream of hot sperm into my warm accepting throat. He continued licking me while I savored the gisarme flavor that he had ejaculated into my mouth. I continued massaging around his thickness as he made me cum again with his mouth for at least the seventh time.

I deeply loved this man so much that I joyfully swallowed every single drop that he ejaculated into my eager stroking warm mouth. I kept licking the juices to his now softer but still impressive penis as he took it out of my mouth and turned around and began mounting me in a prone position on the bed.

I watched with anticipation while his member began getting hard again by revealing the beats of his heart. He held it in his right hand and hovered above me while rubbing the head around the edge of my private lips.

I instantly felt pressure and more juice filled from my out of control passionate acceptance of him into my deepest passion. I screamed out when Joshua suddenly thrust half of his member inside me. I almost passed out from passionate joy when he slowly started to move back and forth going deeper with each stroke. Our lips touched and we both tasted our combined sexual juices as we kissed and made love for a long time with the deepest passion that I'd ever known.

For another hour we were as one while making love in that prone position. Both released several more passionate screams as we endured more pleasure from our ejaculations. We finally collapsed exhausted into a sound sleep somewhere around 2:30 Am in the early morning hours of day 2121 in Unit D-21. Oh My at the 21's.

It was past 10:30 AM on day 2121 before my eyes opened into Joshua's quarters. I covertly left the comfort of his bed and borrowed a suit of his paper clothing to cover my body on the way back to A-7. I softly kissed him on the forehead and left my lover gently snoring as I quietly made my way outside to my waiting transport.

The 40-minute ride home was filled with joyful memories as I was still tingling from thoughts of our lovemaking from hours ago.

Upon arrival I entered my quarters and shed his green clothing and headed straight for the shower.

Never before had I experienced the ecstasy that I had the night before. I realized now that I was totally in love with Joshua Jarvis. I had little sexual experience in my college days but nothing could possibly compare to Joshua's intense lovemaking.

I can't speak for Joshua but in my opinion, I had been to Heaven and back for the first time.

Warm sprinkling water enveloped my body for a half-hour as my right hand again began to wander downward in the soapy lather. In minutes I had achieved another orgasm. Nothing as vigorous as the night before but it certainly felt wonderful to my inner soul.

I knew that the world was to end in six years and all I could concentrate on at this point is the love I had for Joshua Jarvis. I never planned for this to happen. I also never planned for the world to end. Although from first site of Joshua, I was totally hypnotized by his angelic presence.

I was beginning to doubt the possibility that Joshua Jarvis was even from planet Earth. Never in my 37 years on Earth had I ever met such a stunning individual that I was uncontrollably attracted to. For the first time in my life I was totally sexually satisfied. That had never happened until now. Words were unable to describe how I felt. I wasn't complaining. I felt total joyous contentment.

I prepared myself a meal and the rest of the afternoon I relaxed to music and did a few chores preparing for tomorrows report to my workstation.

CHAPTER 17

DBN – 2119 NEW NEMESIS DISCOVERY

A QUICK EARLY stop at the canteen on day 2119 enabled a fresh coffee and pastry breakfast that satisfied my morning energy needs. My thoughts of Joshua and last night's ecstasy adventure were constantly controlling all of my thoughts. To me, it was a life changing experience.

At 7:35 AM my phone alerted me to a call that wasn't immediately recognized. To my surprise it was Joshua wishing me a good start to my workday and telling me how much he enjoyed our lovemaking. Before he hung up he promised to stop by before my work-shift ended today.

I was so glad that he called and for the first time in my adult life I felt loved. A tear oozed from my eye as he admitted that he really loved me. I replied that I love him also.

Lacy Carpenter and Jason Tyler were already at work when I arrived at the dead-end of tunnel Block E. They happily greeted me and immediately began informing me of the dark nemesis's present approaching status. It was now a little over 5 years and 8 months before the black nemesis would arrive at the edge of the solar system. Accurate tracking information revealed that the anomaly's direction and speed was still the same and had not changed.

At my work console I instructed the mountain top telescope to focus towards the Bootes Void. The dark purple spot was still almost invisible but the pinpricks hazy edge had an odd fuzzier tint than before when it was under extreme magnification.

I began viewing the results through a prismatic spectral analyzer that revealed a remarkable new property detail.

Under extreme magnification, the anomaly appeared to be switching from hot to cold temperature variations. How this was possible I didn't know but it surely challenged my perception of the weird properties of this nemesis monster.

Extensive analyzer results revealed that the fuzzy hazy around the black pinprick would disappear momentarily and return a few seconds later. It was if the anomaly was extremely hot for a few seconds and extremely cold when the fuzzy edge returned.

CHAPTER 18

HEARTBEAT OF A MONSTER

I'D CALCULATED TO my best ability and realized that the hottest point occurred approximately every 6.28 seconds. This two-pi resonance frequency was a new weird fact assimilated on my first shift at my new job. How could that possibly be? This far away monster nemesis seemed to have a heartbeat of its own. That was simply an amazing new surreal fact.

Lacy and Jason were now distributing the new learned facts across the world-web to the astronomy society of Earth. I spent most of the day analyzing the new data and around 3:30 I looked up from my station as Joshua stood there smiling.

So pretty lady, how's your first day going so far? Great I replied. I excitably began revealing the new details from the spectral analyzer. I mean the spectral analyzer revealed that the far away black hole has a 6.28 second heartbeat.

What, Joshua shockingly exclaimed! What are you saying?

I'm saying that somehow this black hole is drastically changing its temperature from super hot to super cold on a two-pi resonance of 6.28 seconds. Otherwise, 3.14 seconds after its hottest peak, the fuzzy edge appears and cold temperature reading are way below the cold Kelvin scale.

That's amazing, Joshua injected. Wow! That seems impossible.

I know I replied. But these facts are being distributed planet-wide as we speak and if verified that this new discovery is something that we never dreamed possible.

If the direction and speed remains constant, in 5 years and 8 months it will reach the edge of our solar system. Who knows what could happen to Earth even from that distance.

Joshua's silent reply stepped in and his arms held me tight as he kissed my forehead and said try not to worry; somehow we're going to defeat this monster. I'm committed to remain by your side until eternity begins anew.

His warm embrace and words comforted me and I kissed him softly on his lips. Yes we will be together always I replied. His love is what really made me feel better about the entire upcoming situation. Joshua would become my rock to stand upon over the next five years or so. I loved him so deeply that words were incapable of expressing the deepness of love's spoken reality.

Both of our schedules were extremely busy but after a few moments we made plans to get together again on DBN-2115 before Joshua had to rush off to a board advisory meeting around 8:30 pm that night.

My time with him was so short but I was satisfied of knowing about our future meeting plans on day 2115. In future days, Joshua's office visits became a regular routine that I was totally happy about. In fact, Joshua was not only my passionate lover; he became my best friend over the future days inside the ARC underground Base. Future learned factual details would shock the world even more.

CHAPTER 19

DBN-666
DEVILS DAY ON EARTH

FOR THE NEXT three years and nine months, The ARC project continued with determined haste as the pouring of Abirm continued. Progress was charted daily and at this point was slightly behind on Abirm production.

Humankind's base on the Moon and Mars were well-established accomplishments. Before the discovery of the Monster Nemesis, nations of Earth had endured wars and racist hostilities existed and there was no worldwide harmony for the past several years.

Human space colonies in this time period were as much in danger as anyone on Earth.

The Nemesis was considered to be twice as large as the entire solar system's diameter.

Now around DBN-666, Chaos had escalated in many major areas across the planet. Fires burned in many cities. A majority of humankind's citizens vented their frustrations over the frightening approach of this Monster Nemesis. A lot had died from starvation and violence already.

This devouring dark-monster was now less than a parsec away and was now very visible to the naked eye from the night sky as the earth faithfully rotated away from the Sun.

Looking northeast upon the late night sky revealed a Florissant glowing fuzzy circle of non-light much larger than any bright glowing star in the night sky. Even without a telescope on clear viewing nights

55

the anomaly would appear to the human eye approximately the size of a quarter-coin held at arms length.

Late night news broadcast of day 666, revealed several citywide situations where law and order no longer existed. Worldwide food production had decreased to a point where it was almost impossible for any of the remaining surviving population to feed themselves.

At this point the world situation was getting way worse by the daily rotation period. There were many suicides across the planet.

Breaking news of a nuclear missile strike towards Israel had the entire planet now planning exact measures to handle the situation.

It appeared that certain religious fanatics had envisioned the number 666 as the devils promise to eventually destroy the world.

In all reality, it was human's devilish ways that lead to their own destruction. Possibly a higher power had sent the approaching black hole that was even more destructive than even a real devil could conjure up in his evil mind.

Let my diary state that all of this was certainly a reality that existed in my present time-line.

I celebrated my 37th birthday on May 6th in this year 3025 with my lover Joshua at my designated A-7 quarters. We dined on a feast of many foods as we also partook of the red wine available. We were celebrating tomorrow's special DBN-665 to be our long overdue wedding day. We'd worked together for over four years and were now totally committed to spend the rest of our lives together no matter what the Nemesis does.

Tomorrow Joshua and I were to be married in a private ceremony located at a church inside the base. We'd been lovers for years and we'd finally decided to commit to our remaining days as a married couple. Only our closest friends would attend our secrete wedding on the night of DBN-665.

CHAPTER 20

DBN-665 OUR WEDDING CEREMONY

7-PM Festivities that night consisted of the base pastor and a dozen of our closest friends. We were allowed to have the wedding in the E-blocks private commissary room. Our friends had decorated the lounge with artificial paper flowers of multiple colors and different varieties. If real flowers still existed they just weren't available so everyone improvised the best that was possible.

The decorated room's small size was at its limit with 15 people attending the ceremony. My father had passed away long ago but my friend lacy Carpenter stood in as best girl as we stepped slowly down the isle together. My paper white wedding dress had a colorful trail that swept the floor six-feet behind me as the wedding march played. Lacy held my arm as we marched down the isle to where Joshua and his best man Jason Tyler stood waiting in front of Pastor Graham's podium.

My wedding dress may be made of paper but I can assure you that it would compete with any dresses created in earlier times. Around my neck I wore a bouquet of 7-ROYGBIV colored flowers. Through my gold tinted vale I smiled happily into Joshua's eyes with nervous joy as I made the final step to the music's pause.

Pastor Benjamin Graham officiated the ceremony with raised hands to end the music as the he began the ceremony. He clearly spoke the following words as the room chatter settled down.

Today we are gathered here to join Galena Kay Dresden and Joshua Roman Jarvis in the sanctimonious ceremony of marriage. Any person wishing to speak against this union should speak now or forever hold their peace. There was no objection. Everyone knew that we were in love.

Do You Joshua Roman Jarvis take this woman Galena Kay Dresden to be your lawful wife for better or worse through sickness and health forever? I certainly do Joshua stated starring deeply into my eyes.

And Do You Galena Kay Dresden take this man Joshua Roman Jarvis as your lawful husband for better or worse through sickness and health forever. I certainly do I stated while searching deep into his hazel bluish eyes.

Pastor Graham spoke. Let it be witnessed by the Almighty that the agreement has been made and I now pronounce you man and wife.

You may kiss the bride.

Our lips joined in a sensual kiss for 30 seconds as the wedding retreat march began and we strolled happily down the isle greeted by our friends along the way. I was so proud to marry the man of my dreams. Joshua was all that this woman could ever want. Even though the world was coming to an end. At that moment I felt happy without worry.

CHAPTER 21

THREE-DAY HONEYMOON

NOT MANY PLACES in the world were safe to visit anymore but Joshua and I were allowed a three-day honeymoon at a mountain resort that was considered safe. We were flown by helicopter that night to Bear Valley Mountain Resort in California to spend three days on our honeymoon. We consummated our marriage many times over our stay at the resort. We spent hours together at late night rendezvous in the pool.

I knew now that no matter what happened with the ARC Program, I'd spend the rest of my days with the man that I truly loved. Even until deaths do us part. We danced in the moonlight and shared our happiness together under starry skies. We attempted in vain to ignore the quarter sized black anomaly's existence above our heads in the northeastern sky.

It was late on the third night when we stood holding each other and looking upward at the still far away black monster. We knew that as of tomorrow when we returned to work that there'd only be a year and eight months before the Nemesis reached the edge of the solar system. Our lips met again in a passionate kiss and afterwards we both looked up towards the pulsating black spot.

After making love our finale honeymoon night, we fell asleep in each other's arms and slept sound that night.

CHAPTER 22

RECALLED TO DUTY

DBN-661 BEGAN EARLY the next morning when Joshua's phone alerted us awake to an important call.

We were instructed to report to the resort's helicopter pad by 8:30 AM to be transported back to Cheyenne Base for an important briefing. We hurriedly packed our lightweight luggage and purchased pastry and coffee from the motel's commissary and made our way to an awaiting helicopter. The honeymoon was over.

By 1:30 PM on day 661, we landed at the base only to be rushed to an important meeting with the President of the United States attending.

As the Black Nemesis is now a year and eight months away from the edge of the solar system, only 65 people occupied Cheyenne base with many more to come the following year.

As the briefing began, President Jessica Rogers stepped to the podium to address the gathered group in room E-21 on this early afternoon of DBN-661. She spoke out with concern. Her eyes bore the strain of her tough administration and her aged face bore the results when she spoke.

As of tomorrow's DBN-660, We have a year, eight months and nine days before the Monster Nemesis reaches the solar system's edge. It is extremely imperative that we keep up the dedication of the ARC mission. At this time, I call Joshua Jarvis to the podium to fill us in on the details and progress of the Abirm pour around the base. Joshua Please, she motioned him forward.

Joshua's concerned brow at this point expressed worry of preceding facts of the day. Although his handsome forced smile seemed to assure everyone that all was okay, he began his words with cautious approach of the Abirm subject.

I don't wish to concern anyone he spoke. But in all actually and truth, The Abirm pour around this base is approximately six months behind schedule. With all the destruction already happening across the planet at this present time, there has been some delay in getting the right chemicals and Uranium 235 waste to create enough Abirm. Our production quota is running about 6 months behind schedule.

Quickly he injected his optimist opinion. Please listen though, there's absolutely no need for concern. As it stands now, the pour should be finished eleven mouths before the Nemesis arrives. It takes six months for Abirm to completely get hard so we are still in good shape for the Nemesis arrival date.

I assure you that with all of my ability, that we will finish the pour of Abirm in plenty of time. At this time the base is about 60% encased in the Abirm coating. I just want you to know that we will finish in time to face whatever happens when the Earth is devoured by the Nemesis.

What happens then is anyone's guess. This ARC project is our only hope that we have of possibly surviving this apocalyptic ordeal. With God-speed we move ahead with ARC with all the resources that we can gather. I assure you, completion will be done on time. We will fight this monster until our last breath to make this ARC shelter happen. With that said, I now give you back to President Jessica Rogers for her finale words of this briefing.

Thank You Joshua for all that you are and have been doing to make this project's completion a success. Vice President Jack Norman and myself will join the ARC program about three months before the Nemesis arrives. Twenty—four hours after we arrive, the doors to Cheyenne Mountain will be sealed and no one will be allowed to leave or enter this base.

This project only has the survival capacity of air food and necessities for 169 humans to survive for five years. That's if we can possibly survive such a drastic encounter with total unknowns.

The 169 chosen for ARC are indeed the chosen ones. Including myself, we indeed are the lucky few that even get the chance to try to live past the end of Earth's existence. Those facts to me are what faith and hope are all about. If only one of humanity among us is able to survive, this government has chosen to aspire all of its resources towards the completion of ARC to be encased in Abirm here at Cheyenne Mountain.

I know that you all must have questions but at this point, you know all that I know. Vice President Norman and I and eleven of my colleagues will be joining you here 91 days before Nemesis. I apologize to everyone here but I really must rush off to attend an emergency meeting at NATO in London England.

CHAPTER 23

MORE STUDY OF THE MONSTER NEMESIS

With the President's departure, the meeting was adjourned and we conversed a few minutes among friends before gradually separating to our own duties. Joshua and myself headed for the astronomy lab to seek the latest properties of the Nemesis.

Jason Tyler, Lacy Carpenter along with Joshua and myself arrived at the astronomy base at the end of E Block about the same time. We entered the lab and as a team we began acquiring the latest update on the details of the Nemesis.

The mountain top telescope pointed its direction towards the dark anomaly that was 20 months away.

The fuzz effect still fluctuated with a two-pi resonance from hot to cold every 6.28 seconds. In all of humankind's history, no one had ever thought that anything with mass could do this with the understanding of presently known physics.

After current spectral analysis of the Nemesis we discovered a slight change in its properties. It now would completely become invisible for thirty seconds and return visible for 60 seconds to repeat its two-pi resonance.

This was totally out of context with known physic facts. We had absolutely no comprehension of why this was occurring when the anomaly was still so far away. Then again, we knew very little about the

Nemesis itself. One thing we knew for sure was that this dark monster was headed towards our own solar system.

New facts were being learned daily but tonight's discovery would puzzle scientist even more than anticipated. This dark Nemesis would have even more suppressed facts to reveal as the DBN's get shorter.

Once our team had reported our new discovery to the world astronomy organization, Joshua and I departed to our new assigned larger quarters. Our new assigned quarter was twice as large as our original single quarters. After our marriage we had now been assigned to apartment D-14.

It was past 11 PM before we reached our new quarters. We had a quick snack showered together and made love for several hours before exhausted into a sound night's slumber. I'd decided to change my last name from Dresden to Jarvis and here I rested peacefully my content night at home with my husband Joshua Roman Jarvis in our D-14 quarters. Yes we always lived in fear of the approaching monster Nemesis but moments like these seemed to ease the tension of it all. That was my last memory of DBN 661 before I woke up beside Joshua eight hours later.

CHAPTER 24

DBN 660 TO DBN 234

WE WORKED DILIGENTLY over the next year to monitor the approaching Nemesis. Each day that passed we recorded the precise speed and direction. A year past day 660 we were beginning to discern just how big this approaching monster is. The following year had an extra day due to an added scheduled leap year.

We found ourselves daily infatuated for an entire year with learning as many new facts about the Nemesis as was possible.

Time ultimately passed so quickly before we soon realized by DBN-234 that we were less than eight-months from the Nemesis encounter. Joshua and I ate breakfast and rushed off to a 9 AM presidential meeting in E-Block.

The meeting began with President Rogers calling Joshua to the podium to present the details of the Abirm pour around the base.

Joshua had good news to reveal and stated that the Abirm pour was finished and for the next six months the hardening phase of the poured Abirm will also be complete. That leaves us plenty of time to seal the base doors and prepare for the Nemesis. I'd just like to emphatically state that the president here has informed me that the doors will be sealed on day ninety at 12 noon mountain time.

President Rogers spoke up. That's right, those allowed that miss that closing will not be allowed into the base past the time just stated. Again, that's 12-noon Mountain Time on DBN-90. It's now DBN-234. That means we have 144 days before Cheyenne Mountain will be closed and sealed tight.

We'll all make the best of our research time over this next period of 144 days. Any changes in the program will be notified as they occur.

I as your president am doing the best that I can under these dire circumstances. My sincerest hopes are that we will all work together to allow this ARC project to have a chance of succeeding. I assure each and every one of you that I will certainly do my part.

When it is DBN-91, the Vice President and I and our party of eleven will report here for sealing of the base doors scheduled the following day.

Until that time, I thank everyone as I bid you farewell. Well wishes and prayers to all here today that has worked so hard to make ARC possible.

That ended the Presidential conference on DBN-234 and we all left the conference to attend our duties.

Let my diary reflect, that 7 months and 4 days from the presidential meeting, that we indeed are the chosen ones that are faithfully striving ahead determined to approach the next seven months with as much courage as possible.

This ARC group of 169 humans is the only logical possibility that any human could have a chance to survive the solar system's destruction.

CHAPTER 25

REVOLT OF
THE NOT CHOSEN

IT WAS DBN-126 when Joshua and I over breakfast first learned of the latest perils of humanities resistance to not being one of the chosen ones. Certain defiant media organizations had leaked details of the ARC project to the warring remaining few still alive. On DBN 126 violent caravans of angry survivors were reported heading in the direction of Cheyenne Mountain.

Several troupes of National Guard were at this moment setting up barricades at the base of the mountain to prevent intrusion of the uphill winding road to the base.

Afternoon reports of the first caravan had revealed a fist shaking angry mob of filthy zombie protesters throwing fire lit Molotov Cocktails at the solders that preventing them access to the base from 50 yards ahead of the first barricade.

Angry protesters retreated back to a distance of a hundred yards once the soldiers fired tear gas projectiles towards the crowd. The suffocating gas caused the angry fire-tossing mob to scatter into the brush for temporary safety.

The president had ordered armed helicopter patrols to monitor the uphill perimeter to Cheyenne base and also ordered three more troupes of National Guard to the immediate vicinity of Cheyenne Mountain.

By sunset on DBN-126, another group of National Guard had surrounded the immediate outside perimeter of the base doors. The first of the protesters were controlled but more caravans were reported to arrive, as the DBN's grew closer.

News of worldwide panic and revenge fires had destroyed much of humanities modern city structures. Food supply had dwindled to the point of zombie-starved people scrounging through waste bins for remaining ingestible food particles. Earth as you may have known it didn't exist anymore. There was no hope for so many and only the few involved in ARC had a chance.

Smoke filled skies with almost non-breathable sulfur air hovered over much of Earth's circumference. Dead decaying animals and unburied human remains were stinking up what was left of the surface breathable nitrogen-oxygen atmosphere that hovered like a rusty cloud over many landmasses and filthy shorelines. Shorelines of decayed sea and plant-life engulfed the water's edge of the once beautiful Earth.

Trees and Plant-life had already rejected the new poisonous atmosphere by turning a dark blood red-brown color in their last attempts to survive Earth's changed poisonous air.

Uncontrolled fires burned north and south from the equator towards polar directions. Billions of human beings that once inhabited a healthy beautiful Earth had already perished and no longer existed. Very few vaporous scavenging souls still survived on this now hellish planet.

It was estimated at this point that more than 85% of the entire human population is extinct. Rotting decaying flesh smells filled the nostrils of and surviving surface dweller on the planet.

Earth's ocean surfaces now consisted of floating dead sea-life. Garbage and rotten flesh poisoned the seas near the shorelines of many remaining land masses..

This dying Earth was no longer an Oasis. From space satellites photos, Earth appeared as dirty air world rotating under a sky of red dusty cloud cover. Satellite images distinction between land and water were only possible through infrared radar.

Only a few memories of a bountiful Earth in the remaining human minds exist anymore. With all of that explained, the finale DBN's will be approached with a strict policy of protecting the base in the last days as the Nemesis approaches the solar system's edge.

THE PRESIDENTIAL PARTY ARRIVES

THOSE NEXT WEEKS passed with total chaos happening across the planet. The military had installed an iron dome protection system half way up Cheyenne Mountain.

Members inside the base watched as a massive crowd of militant's fired projectiles toward the base entrance from below the guard's perimeter.

Three air force jets flew very low monitoring the situation preceding the President's arrival at 11:45AM on DBN-91.

President Rogers and her Vice President along with eleven of the President's chosen stepped from the helicopter and were quickly rushed between four saluting guards at the base entrance.

In 24 hours the iron doors of Cheyenne base will be sealed up tight to the outer environment. All that remained outside creatures of any sort will face the approaching black monster with no protection from its wrath of destruction of everything ever known.

CHAPTER 27

DBN-90'S MISSILE ATTACK

Joshua and I were suddenly awoken by loud alarms sounding throughout the base. We both quickly managed to tune into the base's video broadcast. 6:45 AM DBN-90, the base news was broadcasting an immediate emergency.

It was reporting that China and Iran were attempting to launch nuclear warheads at the Cheyenne Mountain complex. By 7:30 that morning, President Rogers ordered NORAD to respond to any missiles that were detected approaching any of the remaining 56 states of America. Condition DEFCON-1 was activated and the president was considering a possible early closing of the main base doors.

President Rogers had immediately called for an 8:30 meeting to discuss the current emergency situation.

By 830 AM about eighty-nine members stood before President Rogers as she began speaking her urgent message.

My sources have informed me that right now, over 60 nuclear missiles from China, Iran and Russia have been launched towards this location. It seems that these angry nations are jealous of the ARC attempt and have decided that if they don't survive the apocalypse then no one will.

The Air force and the dome protection system should be able to neutralize most of the threats but due to these circumstances, I've ordered the base doors to be sealed at 11:00 AM.

Once the base is sealed and locked down, even if there was to be a direct missile strike we should be protected.

I'm asking everyone here to pass the word to please remain calm and be aware that as bad as the situation is that no matter what, we are prepared to deal with it.

CHAPTER 28

SNEAKY MILITARY DOZEN

Twelve Military personnel that surrounded the base door perimeter had conspired secretly to rush into the base as the alarm sounded to seal the base doors. Around 10:50 AM the final alarm sounded and a dozen military guards rushed in before the inner base doors were being sealed to the outside environment. There were eight men and four women that huddle just inside the second sealed metal door.

There was nothing anyone could do about that. They were inside and both inner and outer doors were now sealed to the outside world.

There were now 181 humans locked up tight under Cheyenne Mountain. That's just the facts of that present situation. Those thick doors were closed and come what may, the ARC program was considered launched into the unknowns of the next 90 days and beyond. No one cold change that now. The future was the ultimate destiny of 181 to endure.

It was two hours past the sealing of the base when it was being reported that a nuclear missile had slipped through the iron dome defense and struck the ground two kilometers outside perimeter of the base. Alarms sounded when suddenly the base shuddered slightly.

The Abirm's cocoon surrounding the facility protected the base and life inside felt very little disturbance from the blast.

The first test of the Abirm coating had worked very well. The base had easily withstood a nuclear bunker buster bomb but the real test would come if can survive a massive eating monster black hole that was less than a quarter light year away.

I can imagine in y mind the world abode's burning surface with massive fires shooting skyward and radioactive poison ravaging the remainder of a once breathable atmosphere.

A habitual Planet Earth didn't exist anymore! Land masses and even evaporating gaseous oceans burned as noxious gases merged causing 450 degrees Fahrenheit or 232-Celsius flames of burning poison air to soar several kilometers high above the earth's present charred black surface.

The sneaky dozen that had rushed in were disarmed and put to work in janitorial positions. The 12 had no say in the matter. It was either take assigned jobs or possibly be evicted through garbage disposal back to the poisonous radiation to the above ground non-survivable burning surface and super hot atmosphere.

From A Block to D Block, there were only 160 separate quarters. E block facilities had just enough extra rooms for the Presidential party and a kilometer past those rooms leads all the way to the end of E block tunnel where the astronomy lavatory is located.

The 12 solders had camped out in the hallway way just inside the second door. After spending 48 hours living in the halls of the tunnel they were allowed by the project manager to bunk down in a large machine maintenance room on the left just after you cross A- Block corridor. The twelve gladly accepted the granted accommodation. They were lucky to be here. So were we!

I suppose that if I was not one of the chosen people and I was outside the door when it began closing, I would want to survive also and likely do the same thing that the sneaky 12 did.

By DBN-86, we had all settled in to our duties of monitoring the conditions of the outside world and keeping track of the approaching dark Nemesis.

CHAPTER 29

NO MORE EARTH AS WE REMEMBER

TRAGIC DAYS AHEAD revealed that the once oasis Earth didn't exist anymore. Not because the Monster Nemesis had destroyed the planet yet but it was humankind itself that was the destructive culprit. We were sealed beneath a mountain to the outside world but satellite data from space revealed the ugliness of rotating brown-orange poisoned planet.

It was greed, fears jealously and all of the spiteful human characteristics that ultimately led to the surface world being uninhabitable. Chances of human life existing outside the base were considered to be almost impossible. DBN's passed as we continued to monitor the situation and at this point all seemed well inside Cheyenne Mountain.

As several months passed from the base being sealed, we continuously kept track of the approaching Nemesis. Fires burned all above but somehow the mountain top telescope was still functioning. At 60-DBN, the night stars were already 40% blacked out in huge spiracle blackness towards the northeast night sky.

From DBN-60 to DBN-15, the spiracle blackness grew larger by the day. Two weeks before Nemesis, numerous outside rumbling was occurring. The coating was doing its job but the rumbling of the Earth made us all fearful of the coming event that was now only two weeks from the solar system's edge.

CHAPTER 30

TWO WEEKS AWAY FROM THE UNKNOWN

It seemed to us all that time had passed so quickly since the base was sealed tight from the outside world.

Joshua and I had spent a lot of worried sleepless nights just listening to the rumbling of the planets continents as the gravity of the Nemesis had already began to influence the earth's crust. I remember once waking up in the middle of night on DBN-10 freighted and clutching tightly to Joshua while the walls were vibrating from the gravity stress of the still far away Nemesis Monster.

The vibrations at that point were annoying but tolerable to the soul. The walls had begun emitting soft vibrating sound waves. It was determined that the cause of the vibrations was due to the approaching gravity of the Nemesis. Even at this distance the Nemesis's extreme gravity well was a threat. It's distortion gravity extended way ahead of its physical presence and direction of travel.

In the year 2997 a detection satellite labeled Bata-X had been placed in orbit outside the Oort cloud of the solar system. DBN-7 satellite photos revealed that the trillions of spinning orbiting Ice-chunk asteroids were being ejected from their orbit and pulled toward the approaching Nemesis.

It was DBN-6 when I attempted to activate the mountaintop telescope. It was still working but the night or day view only revealed thick smoggy radioactive atmosphere. Though still operational at this point the telescope was no help at all in monitoring the sky. We soon gave up on the information that the telescope could provide and averted our attention to another resource called Beta-X

On day 6 Joshua and I attempted for several hours to link up with the Beta-X satellite that was hopefully still functional. We couldn't link up for several nights but we were determined to keep trying to break the link-up code. I was only on DBN-3 when Joshua was finally able to break the code to link into Beta-X.

Beta-x was so far out on the edge of the solar system that light wave transmissions took sixteen light hours to travel the distance each way. As soon as Joshua was able to connect he sent a command for the satellite to take pictures and relay them back to earth's remains. We realized that it would be at least 32 hours before we could possibly receive a response. We were desperate to know what was coming our way.

CHAPTER 31

DBN-2 BETA-X'S RESPONSE

The Monster Nemesis was less than 40 hours away from the system's edge by the time we received a response from Beta-X. The far away satellite was stationed at the outside edge of the Oort cloud that surrounds the entire perimeter of the solar system. Pictures were now being received on an hourly schedule and the first photos were of unworldly description.

The anomaly sill resonated with the two-pi resonance from hot to cold on a 6.28 second time period. Every three point fourteen seconds when it was in a hot cycle, it revealed lightning bolts larger than the planet Jupiter. When it presented its cold stage 3.14 seconds later, Gigantic Ice chunk bodies of all shapes and sizes became visible for a few moments.

Shortly after that first connection, all contact with Beta-X was lost. Here we were two days away and no more photos and details would be available. When those few hours of photos had stopped coming, a few more hours passed before the last command was sent to the satellite. Rest in peace Beta-X.

We postulated that by this time, Beta-X had been devoured by the Nemesis or at least overwhelmed by its immense gravity. On the beginning of DBN-1, we were too worried about our own survival to be concerned with what possibly didn't exist anymore.

All we knew at this point was that Beta-X signal was no longer there. We were so close to tomorrow's unknown that we were too worried to even attempt sleep. The entire base was at the mercy of whatever the Monster Nemesis would do. In the past few hours we managed to lock up with another satellite in orbit around Jupiter that at the moment was still functioning.

The first images revealed that Jupiter's entire atmosphere was being sucked towards the outer solar system. A huge long trail of Jupiter's gasses were captured trailing outward towards a black Nemesis that was now very close to the edge of the Oort cloud.

The many moons of Jupiter were already sucked away and didn't exist anymore. We were not able to focus the satellite on Uranus and Neptune due to the satellite's limited range. We assumed that if Jupiter was this destroyed that their ultimate demise was true also.

The Visual of Jupiter with no atmosphere revealed a miniature nuclear brightness as if the remaining surface was a small star. Long range visual from the satellite revealed large chunks of Ice Mountains disappearing as they were gobbled up by the Nemesis. The satellite functioned for another hour before that signal was lost also.

CHAPTER 32

DBN-0 INTO THE UNKNOWN

THE BLACK NEMESIS was now gobbling its way through the Oort cloud and its gigantic gravity well was sucking the matter from the gaseous outer planets way ahead of its arrival. The Nemesis was only 45 minutes from Earth. Most of the 181 souls inside the base had gathered fearfully in block E that is the deepest point under the mountain.

Solid walls inside the base were distorted like wave ripples to the texture of vibrating jelly.

One last thing I remember is launching my diary from the mountain top surface tube in hopes that someday someone will find it and remember that the human race once existed.

Joshua and I embraced each other while glaring deeply into each other's eyes. I've done my best Joshua said. I'll be with you forever and wherever we wind up. His last words that I remember from Joshua's lips were, I'll love you always. I remember telling him that I'd love him forever also as my last words kept echoing through the remainder of my earthly remembered consciousness.

It was like an uncontrollable dream that was impossible to awaken from in this new reality. There was no pain. I had conscious thought but my versions of eyes were unable to focus on what was once my human body.

Indeed I'd never experienced such pleasing brilliant colors as a human. All around me moving orbs existed inside of this new cotton candy consistency that I now also existed in.

A pencil thin circle line bubble containing a square pencil-line inside distinction was my new reality. All of the squared circle beings that now existed here was totally past the comprehension of my once humanly existence.

I had no physical body whatsoever. The pencil thin box marker that was surrounded by a pencil thin circle bubble marking was now all that I existed as in this new reality.

It was as if I existed inside an almost invisible box that was surrounded by an almost invisible protective circle. But the weirdest part was that every 3.14 seconds my circle surrounding would flash and reverberate colored trails behind the direction that I was momentarily traveling. I found myself in a total new unfamiliar awesome gorgeous reality.

Upon realization of my new reality, my immediate thoughts focused on my husband Joshua. I was a bit scared at first. My conscious thought told me that I really wanted my soul mate. I'm not sure why in this new reality but as soon as I was able to think the thought of Joshua, a golden flash appeared near me and instantly I knew it was Joshua's new existence.

Joshua vectored closer and as soon as our circle edges touched, we began communicating. Trillions of other orbs were flashing all around and producing colored trails behind their direction of travel just like Joshua and I were doing.

I felt a super smart warmness as if electricity was vibrating inside my circled bubble. White puffy exotic spaces surrounded each orb that was reflecting soft brilliant roygbiv colors behind their direction of travel.

My first mental question to Joshua was asking if this is what heaven is like? I don't think so Joshua replied. But I do have to admit that this is something so awesome that no human could ever imagine this reality.

I know that it seems as if we are some kind of angelic intelligent being particle but this place is so fantastic that I don't even think that the creator itself could possible turn this situation into our new reality. But who could possibly know of the creator's intentions? Joshua replied.

I assume that no human mind could even fathom such an environment that we exist in now. Earthly words are pitifully incapable of description of this new existence. There was no reality of time passage at all. No air to nourish your non-existent lungs and no liquid blood in our bubble shaped bodies. We weren't humans anymore. That fact was indisputable. What we were now is soon to be revealed.

CHAPTER 33

WHAT I AM NOW

Physics in this reality was nothing like physics that humans endured on Earth.

We had no eyes ears or physical touchable existence at all. All we really had was extreme knowledge of another part of the universe that we could have never thought possible from our post human perspective.

Upon this existence there is no such thing as up and down, right and left or any postulations of ying or yang that any former human might imagine.

Possibly you might describe my presence as atomic but even that description is not sufficient enough to put in words that a former human might come close to understanding.

If I ask a former human how big they were in size, they would possibly respond in their known terms of inches meters or mass. But here, size or mass wasn't relevant at all. There were no winds atmosphere gravity or any solid surface objects that could be touched with a human finger.

We were intelligent beyond human comprehension. We now knew explanations of universal facts that no human could possibly comprehend. The revealed truth was that there were as many universes as there were stars and galaxies in human known terms. We as these beings existed peacefully between universes in a state of perpetual flux. We were the resource building blocks of all of the Creator's possibilities.

Factually, we were now what a human would describe as the stardust of the soul of the Almighty Creator. Think what you will, the creator exist whether you believe it or not. You must think beyond your own existence to know that if you can possibly imagine anything or anywhere at all, that in any one of the Creators universes, it does indeed exist.

I was surprised to remember that humans and many other biological creatures at one time were like seedlings to grow past their existence to eventually evolve into what I exist as now.

Relationships like I had known with Joshua on Earth were remembered but not necessary in this new environment. I knew he was available should I require communication but here in this universe, deeper thoughts were the main reason for all of our existence.

I personally knew that the entire population here of beings such as myself, would be immeasurable by human terms. I also know that we existed as a whole together for a specific reason. That reason was the Almighty Itself. We were now the atoms and stardust of the Almighty's soul.

We surged though the inner veins like photons in a light beam. But you must understand that to a human being, we would not be visible or detectable. Indeed the collective intelligent beings that we surely are, most definitely does exist. These beings such as I am now, always have existed through out eternity.

CHAPTER 34

MY NEW PURPOSE

H ERE I AM simply one of innumerable colored flashing pencil lined Orbs that exist in this universal plain of cold to hot on a two-pi resonance count. I have no humanly feelings what so ever. I do have knowledge of past humans of Earth but these memories are irrelevant to my purpose of why I exist now.

My purpose now was to translate my immediate area's hot to cold temperature every 3.14 seconds in sequence with the innumerably population of my new species. That was the purpose of all the orbs. Dark matter Orbs were indeed a single entity race. Here we were all the same.

We were what humans always postulated about but could never comprehend or discover. Humans would have referred to our kind as invisible dark energy with absolutely no ideal of what we actually were. It was so complicated that humans could have never located or potentially described the properties of our black ion race.

Dark energy such as us black ions are what the majority of the vacuum void of space is made from. Humans would describe my universe as a void vacuum of nothingness. That's not even close to the truth. The environment that I exist in now is what long ago caused the creation of the existence of space itself way before the human term of a big bang solution.

This was a repulsive space-place that universes could be born grow ejected and prosper. In other words, We Orbs as a humongous society of invisible to human species are responsible for the space that everything exists in. We are the dark energy beings. We are Orbs of Repulsive Dark Energy that make up space itself.

No matter where you were along your human life preparedness for this next existence, dark energy always will and always did exist all around and through you.

I again ejected the heat from my purpose and for 3.14 seconds of coldness I pondered the meaning of it all. All of the Orbs around me did the same in Unisom. We jointly knew that because we exist so does the space that holds all matter.

Star matter to us was just an annoyance to the space that we create for matter to exist.

We as an individual Orb's are capable of understanding the laughable idea that in our past human existence we considered ourselves to be the only intelligent life form known to exist. That reality is so far from the truth that even I could relate to the laughable humor now that I had been converted into a Dark Matter Orb.

I am what I am and nothing could change that fact.

The ponderous thoughts of how it all began exist deep in the cold pi side of my progressive collective thinking.

From this point on, I am capable of movement and new exploration. Although my collective intelligence was enormous, I still possessed the ability to ponder about things yet unknown by the collective.

Usually my wondering was immediately explained by another Orb that already knew the answer. So, I as an individual Orb decided to ponder a question that I had always wanted answered.

CHAPTER 35

MY PONDER TO THE COLLECTIVE

TIME HERE WASN'T measured or even relevant to how long it took me think of and decide what my first ponder to the collective would be. I after much deep thought came to the conclusion that it would be as following but I first started my ponder with a statement of agreed known facts.

I know that we all are essentially the hidden dark mater particles that pulsates though the veins of the Creator. I'm also positive that as insignificant as we are as individuals, collectively we are the energy blood of the Creator. My ponder to all is this.

If I were to use the vision that I once had when I was a human being, how would I envision a characterization of what the Creator would appear like in human visual terms?

Time wasn't relevant here but if you must understand under human terms how long an answer took. It was more like a Pluto orbital year of silence before a replay to my ponder was addressed by a very old Orb of the Collective. (BTW) It takes 90,560 earth days or little over 248 former Earth years for Pluto to Orbit the Sun one time. That amount of time didn't mean anything here. The reply was given after a long collective collaboration among all Orbs.

His answer as stated by my allowed ponders. Human eyes are not capable of visually seeing the face of the creator. Any kind of flesh would be instantly vaporized within quadrillion's of kilometers away from the creator. Your Ponder is not unreasonable so I will attempt to explain further details.

In the beginning of everything, there existed a great void. Space itself did not exist yet. What humans referred to as the great void was after the real void existed. So, the creator first made our likeness of black repulsive Orbs and multiplied us in vast quantities and distributed us evenly throughout the real void that from that point on the black Orbs have always represented the true properties of space itself.

The creator knew that first an Ocean had to be created to manifest the creator's future creations upon. This ocean was space. The creator first made an unlimited omega amount of space to have a place to construct atomic matter from the original heavy dark Orbs.

As the creator squeezed the original black orbs together it began the process of creating hot magnetic matter across the entire newly created place it called space. Eventually this coalescence of mater created galaxies of stars, planets, moons and much left over debris scattered everywhere as the space that was first created from dark energy Orbs was always expanding and creating matter while always pushing it outward towards infinity.

All of these processes were necessary in order to get to the stage of biological proliferation of many such organic species. It was the first starlight and planetary goldilocks zones around stars that allowed waters to be liquefied and photosynthesis for plant-life to feed the later evolving biological creatures such as animals and humankind.

With the aforementioned accomplished, the creator then dispersed many species of intelligent life onto quadrillions of worlds that had eventually cooled into oasis planets of many breeding possibilities. The Older Orb explained all of this through the continual and then in conclusion reverted back to my original ponders.

There is no possibility of any human or biological animal flesh being within zillions of kilometers of the one and only omnibus creator. There is a limit of distance that biological life can approach. The creator is not a person as you may envision. The creator is indeed a spirit being of extreme powerful wisdom.

Yet stated as known, the miniature likeness atoms of the creator exist deep inside every common known matter particle that has ever existed even way before the beginning.

However, the Creator itself was amused by your ponder and decided to send you on a journey to within a safe distance for the Creator to explain in voice more details to the answer of your amusing ponder. The Creator's order has been issued. Your journey begins.

CHAPTER 36

JOURNEY TOWARDS THE CREATOR

IN AN ORB 2-pi flash, I changed into a moving dark beam accelerating so fast my dark energy beam was warping space ahead of my travel and it was if my essence was being sucked deeper inside the Dark Bootes Void along my impossible to measure time's journey towards the Creator's allowed boundary.

I had learned from human knowledge that the ultimate speed that a light beam or photon could travel in a vacuum was approximately 186,282 thousand miles in one-second of human measured time.

That being true in human terms meant nothing to the dark beam that propelled me forward towards a far away destination unknown.

I surmised that I must be traveling 2-pi times the speed of light.

That being true means I was traveling 1,168,080 miles per. second inside the Bootes Void for a time-span of at least a thousand Pluto Orbits in human measured terms.

Time had no meaning anymore. Speed and distance had no limit. Only my finale chosen destination awaited my arrival from far away. I controlled nothing of my journey. The creator awaited my arrival from a distant universal environment that would surprise any human mind.

It was the distance between a million universes that I traveled at well over a billion miles each second. I'm not sure that a human's brain can possibly imagine the darkest of dark space travel towards a remarkable feature now becoming slightly visible in the far ahead distant purple blackness.

Now only halfway past my already long journey a mere tiny spec of exotic colored brilliance was slightly visible if viewed in human eye terms?

I focused my view on the amusingly brilliant pinprick of glorious light that existed far ahead of my vectored journey. What ever it is appears to be the only visible obstacle far ahead of my intended final destination.

A human might possibly measure my time of travel as a billion Pluto orbits but distance already traveled would be impossible to rationalize with their base ten-math system.

Zeros past infinity would be required multiplied by the power of infinity.

That vast distance is unexplainable in actual distance traveled but knowing that I still had 47% of distance already traveled was very helpful in understanding that I still had a long distance to traverse on my journey towards the Creator's allowed approach.

In a hypnotized wisdom slumber I faithfully followed my vector of travel for what a human would describe as eons. Time represented no comprehension to me any more as I knew I was riding a dark wave of power towards the direction of the Almighty. I was proud to be chosen. I journey patiently faithfully onward.

The fuzzy odd shaped visual at this distance was almost impossible to describe in human words. It was still so far away but nothing else was visible in the circumference of the vast amount of space that the Creator occupied.

Many more earth years passed before a better description became available to relay. To put it more clearly, let me just state that what I was actually seeing in the far distance would not be visible to human eyes. A better description was, in the blackness that surrounds the creator. There was a spectral green mystified fuzzy anomaly that human words seemed incapable of description.

My new existence was like a newborn child that was trying to comprehend infinity. Yet I understood that upon arrival to the creator's allowed edge, I would know why this was a reality way past my ability to comprehend nature's surprises. My patience was strong as my long journey proceeded with the passage of eons unrelated to when I might arrive. I knew that I would arrive eventually. That's all that mattered.

CHAPTER 37

A PARSEC FROM THE CREATOR'S EDGE

Eventually as miles passed at over a billion miles per second, I arrived within 5% of the Creator's allowed edge. This close to the edge I was surrounded by a protected shell provided by the creator itself. In another century of human measured time I arrived at the very edge of the allowed distance.

No human matter known would ever be allowed to get this close to the creator's edge. The creator existed well over a parsec awayfrom where I was allowed at the edge of durability.

A parsec is equal to 3.26 light years distance. The distance that a beam of light travels in one earth year is approximately 5.8 trillion miles.

A light beam travel in a parsec times 3.26 light years would equal well over 19.2 trillion miles or about 30.9 trillion kilometers.

I existed inside my bubble at a distance of over 20-trillion miles away from the creator and the experience I was having at this instance of non-time was beyond humanly words of explanation. I was controlled and commanded by a soothing voice from the creator to stop approaching. I complied and remained stationary awaiting further response from the creator.

I was under the influence of a more powerful presence than I could ever possibly imagine. The black outlined orb that I represent existed only in miniature in a state of rosy-golden flux as the creator began addressing my ponder. Visual wasn't allowed due to burning rays of blue-green radiation extremely brighter than any human could endure.

Mystical bell toned communications from the creator echoed through my existence. Heavenly musical voice tones were translated to me through soft musical tones that were instantly transferred into my knowledge of understanding.

Exotic musical tones being played were immediately translated to understanding principals of whom I knew nothing of before this fascinating encounter. The Creator's musical tones continued translating explanation of the reality and actual physical nature of the creator's very own existence.

CHAPTER 38

TRANSLATION OF THE CREATOR

EACH MUSICAL NOTE tone revealed a wealth of information about the creator. It was explained that the creator's genetics were saturated in all things from Alpha to Omega. Before anything else ever existed the creator always existed even before human known beginning. According to the Creator, there was no such thing as before. Its presence was the instantaneous reality of all time present or past at any instance of human measurable terms.

Everything that exists in the entire mega millions of universes is the spiritual mass creations of this lone creator's imagination and abilities. The Creator is not made of physical matter like a human would describe. The Creator is indeed a vast powerful spiritual manifestation of extreme knowledge and power control to all that is possible to be known already exist in the creator's omnibus vast mind.

As a parsec sized plasmatic spiritual being the nothingness that it once knew never existed and all things were invented and created by its extreme power that is non comprehensible by human standards.

Explanations continued in each music tone at a speed so immense that human comprehension would be incapable of knowing the extreme reality of the Almighty's words of wisdom. But to explain in human terms to the best of my new-formed ability, I will indeed try.

Humans of earlier times understood that atoms exist in all things known. The creator itself contained dark energy atoms of a kind that humans were incapable of understanding this disguised hidden fact.

That said, if you imagine how many atoms exist in the makeup of a single grain of sand compared to the amount of atoms that exist inside a human body, you might begin to understand the unique complexity of the spiritual creator's virtual properties.

The creator's atoms are compressed so tightly that the creator itself represented repulsion throughout all known universal existence. Yes there were many collisions that continuously occur but such collisions were always at the direction of the creator's constructive will.

All of the innumerable amount of galaxies, planets and stars, are the storage capacitors connected to the creator's awesome power.

If not for the storage of power existing in many universal creations, the creator would not be able to procreate life under any circumstance that humans are capable of knowing.

In an example of one grain of sand among all the beaches in the universe, in on grain of sand the creator stores enough power to propel an entire solar system with planets past light speed towards the outer unknowns with a single wishful thought.

Imagine the power that the creator possesses through all universal matter uncountable that the creator created across all of the quadrillions of multiverses.

The Almighty Creators amount of stored energy itself is what causes the repulsion of new infinity space that the creator itself lives inside of its own entirety entity.

The environment where the creator resides has a perimeter boundary that exists where created matter is repulsed outward and cannot occupy any space inside the creator's 3.26 light year boundary.

The only exceptions allowed inside the creator's immense diameters are the condensed dark matter atoms of the creator's own master circulatory system.

Inside the reverse rubberized environment of the creator's secretions, are ejections of an outward repulsive force that continuously creates all the new space for all new universes to contentiously keep expanding.

The creator has no physical body of any sort except the repulsive nature of its own state of existence. The Creator is the I am of all things possible. Its own existence is why everything else exists.

It is not but if it were possible to display in vision the appearance of the creator in human terms, it would be like an ant trying to visualize and describe the appearance of a huge dinosaur from well below the surface of its toenail height. Even that scale comparison multiplied a trillion times wouldn't equal the reality of the creator's omnibus presence.

In the Creator's reality, imagine that the ant dinosaur analogy wouldn't equal anything close to describing the creator's physical size. Take the math and size difference between an ant and dinosaur and multiply that answer a sextillion times pi and even that wouldn't come close to the size of the creator.

Now that that attempted description was offered, the Creator addressed the reason that it created humans, as I knew them. In that answer I indeed was very surprised by the change in tone of the notes frequency reply. The tone changed from harp like to a whimsical melody of fascination as the creator defined the reason for human existence.

Let me be assuring in my response that there are many worlds that I created for survival of humanoid entities throughout many of my universes. In humans of planet earth, I attempted to create a peaceful garden where humans could procreate and prosper. In the beginning, human knowledge of astronomical physics and mathematical equations wasn't necessary. Alternately in human creation, I instilled an excessive amount of curiosity for learning and always wanting more knowledge. Humans endured and progressed over time to always understand new things within their own reasoning or postulation.

Humans grew in knowledge to the point that they had the ability to destroy things of my creation including the beautiful world that I created for them to live and prosper.

As the creator, I postulated many times about destroying humankind over their foolish wars and corruption. Many years I watch greed over rule common sense when ultimately, as you now know, I could not resist the corruption of humans-kind anymore.

It was I the creator who had finally come to the conclusion that the evil in humans out weighed the good that I originally intended.

It was I the creator who sent the dark nemesis to delete humankind and recreate better humanoids in another form.

Although certain minds of former humans might consider me as an evil creator, that is quite the contrary of the real truth of my being.

I the creator created all things. In instances that I do destroy one of my creations, it is certainly for the purpose of recreation for the betterment than it ever was before. To that asset of my abilities, I have always remained true to creations.

I am the creator. Creation is and has been my unlimited destiny. No one or nothing else can create as I do. The creator paused in its response but assure me that it was only allowing me time for assimilated facts so far exposed.

I as a feeble black outlined orb was totally infatuated by all that was exposed of reality at this point. The paused silence of the creator allowed me a moment to wonder if all that I had learned so far was all there is to know of the creator. In that wonder of the moment it turned out that I was totally wrong about the creator. There was indeed way more knowledge to be gained from the existence of the creator and everything else. I soon found out that the creator was much more glorious than any human could possibly imagine.

The creator's response resumed periodically as to another ponder that I wished upon it on how the creator itself came into existence. A serious musical toned replay translated into instant words of wisdom.

Here as I am now, has always existed even before any atomic yielding particle ever existed. There is never a moment that I cannot remember of my existence. There are moments of first knowing that until your ponder was asked that I as the creator had never considered.

I am certain that I have always existed where I exist now. To answer your ponder about anything existing before Alpha, The only thing that existed before Alpha was I the Creator. I have always existed and I always will.

CHAPTER 39

TERRA GAIA AND ENHANCED HUMANS

I SURMISED THAT the creator was proving its point by allowing me to visualize my future new world that it had recently created for the next version of human's to evolve without corruption of morals and common sense ideals.

I was instantly whisked into a unique new consciousness of a beautiful world environment that I gleaned from the creator's reference, as it's recent creation called Terra Gaia.

On this new world all the resources that an enhanced human could possibly ever need was easily acquired on the creator's new version of a better world for human beings.

This two-moon glorious water planet promoted the betterment of humans and animal kind and enlisted the destruction of all the evil greed and anger from the former humans characteristic behavior. Stress on this world didn't exist among the new human Terra Gaia society.

The Creator was allowing me a temporary virtual journey to the surface of Terra Gaia as I began to envision the most beautiful serene world that I could possibly dream up in my imagination.

Standing as a human upon peaceful shores I was allowed to breath through human lungs the fresh oxygenated atmosphere and absorb the richness of sounds from new kinds of nature's creatures that would be unfathomable to any former human mind.

Incredibly beautiful glowing reflecting feathered fowl sailed underneath higher rich pale rosy clouds. Bountiful animal life upon land was even more fascinating to behold. Momentarily in a received retrieval message from the creator, I was able to view a brand new version of human beings that was more perfect than anything imaginable.

The new humans of Terra Gaia were not bound by the percentage of gravity than a human once endured on earth. Humans here moved around in a manner unrelated to former humans. Their facial craniums were fifteen percent larger and body appearance was in a form unrecognizable by former human standards.

Longer arms and six fingered hands allowed their base twelve math system to easily allow comprehension of their forward thinking scientific accomplishments.

New humans moved around methodically in a lighter gravity environment collectively tasked to a unique intended directive each with their own assigned task.

Their collective single intended purpose was to create a better world to exist upon. In their minds were no such thoughts of war, poverty, death or corruption. Their collective goal was to exist together peacefully with an intentional scientific combined purpose.

A single new human governing leader was an individual elected for one term by the populace every ten of their years or 100 orbits of their larger Moon.

The elected leader's ideal purpose was to make Terra Gaia the best place for present human life and all of the animal and plant life to exist without possibility of corrupt or misguided intentions.

It was not if the leader were a dictator king or queen as a former human would know about. The leader was advised by the public regularly if any serious issues needed addressing. There were not many problems here on this peaceful planet.

Terra Gaia has no separate nations or nationalities. Terra Gaia has gorgeous green oceans that circled 7 larger separate landmasses. Many rosy-green populated islands surround the seven landmasses.

Forty percent of the largely nitrogen based lower atmosphere was saturated with what humans would refer to as hospital pure oxygen.

During the short period of my allowed visit I concluded that their present galvanized goal was to solve a very serious medical health issue that was fatal in certain newborns.

That medical anomaly was their present world contributed goal of an issue that desperately needed to be solved. There was indeed much peace and harmony among the population of new humans. There was absolutely no strife to endure whatsoever.

New humans of Terra Gaia all spoke the same language that was translated for my understanding. Every human with the exception of the elected leader was equal in status.

The elimination of money erased the want and greed from the hearts and minds of new human beings. There was no need for a political police force to watch over the citizens. There was no such thing as crime at all. Only cordial language and a large quantity of volunteer service existed everywhere among the new humans of Terra Gaia.

Terra Gaia was much smaller in diameter than planet Earth. Measured by human standards, the planet's diameter was approximately 6,300 miles.

Terra Gaia with its two moons is a new oasis world existing as the third of seven planets in this remarkable solar system.

Terra Gaia is an amazing world that orbits its class G star named Tau Ceti at a distance of approximately eighty-seven million miles with an axle tilt of 18.6 degrees.

Terra Gaia's has a moon named Odessa with a diameter of a thousand miles or 1600 kilometers and also a small 150-kilometer diameter moon named Bella that orbits very close.

Odessa orbits 18 times in a Terra Gaia year, which would take 10 months in former earth measured time.

It takes Terra Gaia 296-former earth day's to orbit its star called Tau Ceti. The Odessa-moon orbits above Terra Gaia from about 197 thousand miles every twenty-five days measured by former earth standards. The Odessa moon orbits Terra Gaia a little over 18 times in Terra Gaia's one-year orbit.

Terra Gaia's present technology had brought society past the want to destroy their world with nuclear bombs and wars that kill and destroy. That kind of human mentality had never occurred on Terra Gaia. Everything that every single human needed was provided. No human was ever in want of any single thing. That was the personal friendly sane nature of the new humans of Terra Gaia.

It appeared to me that the creator had removed all the bad traits of past human nature and replaced it with the ability of only clear logical thinking. That fact I adamantly agree with. If only the humans of my former earth could have known the truths and beauty of such a world as Terra Gaia.

I now surmise that it was the fact humans from my former time weren't capable of fixing their own shortcomings and that was the main reason that the creator decided to intervene and create a better world and better human being society.

CHAPTER 40

CREATOR'S MUSICAL WISDOM

I CONSIDERED MY visit to Terra Gaia way too short but I wasn't in control so quickly without warning I was whisked away back to the Creator's boundary limit and patiently awaited further contact. It would seem that a day to you and I verses the Creators day would be an unreasonable conclusion.

In the creator's mind, the measurement of time didn't ever exist and the Creator always has existed without a measurement of the passage of time. To the creator, time was static and the present moment was all that mattered. Eventually after many Pluto orbit periods, the creator spoke these words of wisdom to me through translated musical tones.

Humanoids of any sort or any atomic particles are my reason for ominous spiritual existence. I as the creator can admit to short comings of certain creations. I always endeavor to correct shortcomings of any of my creations. That is why the essence of humans was changed to populate Terra Gaia for a better human existence.

Attitudes of greed, corruption and criminal activity no longer exist for the betterment of humans that now populate Terra Gaia. To be accused of a crime in this new human society of Terra Gaia would actually be a crime in itself because there is no such thing as crime on human's new world.

The creator revealed the fact that it had given warnings to former earth-humans many times that money and greed is not what was intended for humans to worship. The grand oasis earth that the creator had given them to dwell eventually became so polluted that the atmosphere was not healthy for any animal or plant life to breathe.

So much of human kind had begun to worshiped greed and money, which had become the root of all evil.

To the better humanoids of Terra Gaia, I have created better humans and provided a new world to dwell without corruption. It is now left to their own destiny to be able to grow and mature as logical beings.

It was the intention of I the creator to create good humans in the beginning but my shortcoming of allowing evil for so long was indeed not my original intension. Thus the creation of Terra Gaia for a better human existence is my remedy.

The finale musical toned expressed wisdom to me with also a assured commitment towards me of extreme future happiness.

That promise seemed very interesting to me in the moment but I really had no idea or ability to comprehend what it could possibly mean to me personally. I suppose that's because at this moment I was a obscure black ion orb and not a human at all.

I was simply a mere inquisitive black-outline orb.

The creator's will power put me into a deep hypnotic slumber and all that I remembered after that point was that at one time when time was relevant, I once existed as a former human being from a planet whose name was intentionally erased from my memory.

Eventually most memories of that existence were gone and I awoke beside my husband at our home outside Newtown on continent number three of the Terra Gaia human collective.

Could it all have been a dream? I was convinced that I had been in the almighty presence of the creator. Yet I only had realizations of always living here on Terra Gaia. As groggy as I was, I was startle by a cry from our newborn daughter from the next cubicle of my futuristic room.

I easily glided in low gravity to her side in this 68% gravity world I almost instantly held her warmly in my cradled arms. My husband

Joshua and I had named her Miracle Michel Jarvis and in my opinion there has never been a more beautiful baby born.

Joshua entered the room and snuggled us both from behind and kissed us each upon the forehead. I love you both more than a quadrillion Odessa moon orbits around Terra Gaia.

I chuckled at his analogy and immediately tuned and kissed him passionately before replying with a new word on this world that somehow popped into my mind I'll love you always even until the end of time.

Joshua looked at me so straggly surprised at the use of the word time that he'd never heard before.

What is this word called time Joshua asked? There's no such word as time. Present moments in all individually occurring before proceeding moments are all that there is to assimilate.

On Terra Gaia, instant moments are all that matters as a measurement. Indeed we have excellent past moment recollection but on our world there is only daylight of shadow of Terra Gaia's rotation period that there is any need of such past moment recollections. There is no required need of such measurements as the mind of an ancient human might assume.

Everything on this world is as simply as each progressing moment. That's simply the way that it has always been on Terra Gaia. I could only smile at his response instantly realizing that is indeed the way the creator felt.

As the next moments passed in our conversation, I didn't know how such a weird word as time actually slipped from my lips but I knew that the creator being real was a undeniable truth. I was if the word time was a spoken word clue to the instant reality of the Creator.

All on Terra Gaia worshiped the creator. Secondly each new human respected and worshiped each other. As a couple we are so thankful that we are the creators of Miracle Jarvis the most precious child possible to Joshua and Myself.

Love between couples on this world was a respectful stress less way of enjoyable life. Humankind's new world through collective cooperation of methodic order indeed has a fascinating future full of unique possibilities for the new human race.

CHAPTER 41

OUR NEW HUMAN LIFE UPON TERRA GAIA

I IN THIS new life only had memories of my present life here on Terra Gaia. I knew now that I grew up here with a wonderful mother and father with two siblings as twin males that were younger than myself.

I awoke early that beginning of star shine on Terra Gaia attending to my regular duties of being the mother of a newborn infant. The reality of this world bare no evidence of the past human earth drama experience. The female baby I held had exceedingly well mentality much improved from the humans of past earth history. Earth reality was no longer remembered and I had no evidence that kind of corrupt humans ever existed.

The beautiful child I held in my arms was the entire reason for Joshua and my self's present existence. My husband Joshua and I dwelled happily in our trapezoidal shaped home. At the very top was my triangular shaped astronomy observation peak that presented openness to the night skies during shadow periods. The lower levels were our two stories living quarters of our Gaia tree constructed material home.

Trees on this planet were nothing like the trees that a former human could conceive. A rich oxygen atmosphere content and low sixty-eight` percent former earth gravity, allowed trees to grow different than a former human of earth could describe as a tree's appearance.

The majorities of Gaia Tree's grow up to 60-meters tall and were farmed for processing many items of this world. Gaia wood when processes and consolidated and infused with Gaia-bee polymer, produces an opaque glasslike material that many buildings and many other products were made of.

Under the green skies of non-shadow period, buildings and homes reflected very brilliant rainbow spectral colors to their immediate vicinity. A former human couldn't possibly imagine the beauty of such surface structures under green speckled starlit skies of Terra Gaia.

As soon as I had attended my motherly duties and assured of Miracle's wellness, I hugged and kissed both her and my husband and proceeded to transport to Newtown to get supplies and necessities.

My acrylic-wood oval door opened to fresh oxygenated air as I stepped outside among yellow grass just passed the umbrella style front deck. Each of the four gliding steps that I took brought me a meter closer to an egg-shaped oval opaque transport that floated 6 centimeters above a glasslike parking surface. The vehicle was fully charged and upon approach a center oval door opened to allow me access. Transportation glide ways on Terra Gaia were made from opaque acrylic-wood.

Inserted below all roadways were electrically charged modulating magnets that would match up to a separate modulating magnetic plates on the vehicles bottom to attract or repel the vehicle along the glide way.

These hybrid transports also had charged back up electrical motors for instances when the vehicle was off the electric magnetic glide way.

I floated along freely ten centimeters above dark glasslike magnetic glide paths towards my destination called Newtown Continent Three that was approximately 10 kilometers distance along the northbound magnetic freeway.

Polarized visions above my head inside the transport entailed green skies with purple and pink clouds that would be any artist aspiration to paint upon a canvas.

A purplish Odessa moon was visible setting in the western sky as the golden star shine was beginning early in its 15-hour cycle. Open fields on both sides of the glide ways revealed huge elongated fields of yellow food crops used to feed the new human population.

The foods ingested by humans consisted mostly of a products made from Mana-seed. Mana-seed itself was a very remarkable creation by the Creator. Easily grown in the rich oxygen atmosphere of Terra Gaia, Mana-seed produced a golden yellow two-meter tall crop full of all the vitamins and nutrients that humans of Terra Gaia could ever need.

Once harvested, Mana-seed was made into many different varieties of delicious foods. The favorite drink was made from highly hydrogenated water that was excellent for human health issues and long life spans.

Newtown's placement along the shoreline revealed floating vessels powered by wide underwater magnets a half-kilometer below the water level that attracted and repelled ships along their way between all seven continents.

Everything this society has done is activated upon the premise of a betterment of human life and the protection of Terra Gaia's precious for humankind ecosystem.

Former human words are incapable of describing the beauty here from the surface. As far as I knew, I was born here and my many Terra Gaia orbits had been my entire life so far.

It takes my world ten of the former earth months to orbit its Star. My lifespan memory of my present age was 450 orbits of the Odessa moon that orbits Terra Gaia. orbits. I surmise that if you convert that to former earth value, I would be 37 and a half earth orbits old. But here I was considered 450 orbits of age. Age on this world was best described as Odessa's moon orbits.

A healthy life span on my world has been recorded to be as many as 15,000 star orbits. That would equate to 1,250 former earth years. The entire population at this point was approximately three and a half billion humans.

In about ten minutes of earth value time, my transport delivered me silently to the shopping destination that I had earlier programmed into a finger touch floating computer screen. The shoes I wore on my feet allowed me magnetic levitation of controlled push and repel of the walkways and necessity shop floors.

I glided my cart ahead as I made my way slowly down the isles of the shop called Odessamart. Here all foods were stored alphabetically among rows a meter and a half tall with 90-meter long isles. The opposite side of the market displayed isles of any kinds of hardware that a human could ever require.

This one huge market had all things that a human could possibly need. It was recorded upon my exit all the products I had chosen. This was only for restocking purpose because no such thing as monetary money ever occurred in my transaction. Money was never needed on Terra Gaia. There was no such thing as money.

Humans upon this world volunteered for their work interest and this allowed them time of their choosing to investigate other interest of their own. This collective process comes together to produce a healthy productive life-style society.

I loaded my shopping choices in the back compartment then fastened my belt and programmed the transport to take me back home. Silently I lifted up 6 more centimeters and sailed south along dark glasslike glide ways under spectral colored skies.

I wanted to hurry to get home but safety here was the first protocol of humanities travel mode.

My transport took me through a short mild shower of Gaia rain that caused the effect of refreshing the air all around as I stepped outside my transport near our doorway to greet my husband Joshua.

Our daughter in his arms smiled through shaded glasses at me when Joshua transferred her to my reaching gentle grasp. Miracle our child was only two Odessa orbits old and was already attempting understandable phonetic language. She was the joy of our life. Joshua and I planned to have one more child hopefully a son to follow his male kind. Most couples on Terra Gaia averaged two children per family although there were exceptions.

I had arrived back home in time to fix Joshua a quick morning meal before he had to rush off to his volunteer professor job at Newtown

University. I loved Joshua deeply and suspected after last shadow's lovemaking session, that he may have already impregnated me with his future hopeful son. I felt fine but there's a next day feeling that only a female could relate to. I had that feeling.

As soon as Joshua left for his volunteer duties I showered and prepared the baby for her daily routine of learning activities.

I activated a robotic baby watcher as I grabbed my identification and entered the transport to lift me up to the top of my dwelling's astronomical observatory.

I volunteer during shadow periods to study planets and rogue asteroids. I was merely here momentarily to set computer programs in preparation for tonight's upcoming shadow period.

It took me a few moments but I soon accomplished setting the computer program to the co ordinance of the sky that I wanted to view after starset. After starset the brilliant rings around Terra Gaia's equator gained stunning prominence in the upward view towards space.

Verification complete I return to the side-transport to lower me to our living quarters. In a few bounced steps inside I proceeded to the baby's room to relieve the robotic baby tender and held my child and spoke mama words to the beautiful soul that I was holding.

To Joshua and myself all things were special but to both of us, little Miracle meant more than life itself.

The queasiness in my stomach was telling me that possibly I might have great news to share with Joshua when he gets home from his volunteer professorship starlight duties.

Volunteer workers on our world performed their duties for half rotation time during star shine periods.

Shadow time was priority of choice for many volunteers such as myself. As an astronomer, I enjoyed my shadow time service duties during the 15 hours shadow cycle of our ringworld moonlit darkness.

The universe that I recorded was so grand and awe inspiring that I was extremely excited to always have the duty of searching the heavens to discover new phenomena occurring.

Our happiness together was indeed very intense. In fourteen more of our moon orbits Joshua and I were blessed with the birth of our precious son that we named Joshua Jarvis Jr. I suppose that would equate to 11-mouth gestation period in former earth times. Possibly the creator needed more present non-linier moments to create a better human than the original.

Time here on Terra Gaia was only equated to each present moment. There is no need to let occurrences of the past to possibly influence present planetary circumstances.

Thoughts of future rotations were only important to each human's rotational progress in life. Scientific studies were made to solve any potential issues that might possibly happen. Total logic was their guide to the common sense approach of understanding nature as their world uniquely provides.

There is no such thing as pain on our world. Joshua and I like many other couples were at each moment overwhelmed with contentment and happiness.

Private participation with other couples gave us courage to succeed and offer sufficient logical advice to deal with trivial non-important issues.

We the better made humans that occupy Terra Gaia's seven continents and multiple shore line islands, will always work diligently like bees in a hive for the betterment of all-life on our paradise planet made by the creator.

On the world of Terra Gaia, existence and happiness is not about money or golden treasures. It's about a society of peaceful equals that strive for the betterment of their planet. Their main narrative is emphasized with a strict directive towards the protection of all planet wide life forms on this new brave world.

No form of currency is needed on Terra Gaia. The only reason for recording any product is for restocking purposes. I suppose that in former earth thinking terms one might even surmise that everything on this world was absolutely free. Indeed it is. Every adult human has a volunteering job interest and laziness is irrelevant or non-existent.

All of the needs that any citizen might have are easily provided without question. A devastating ancient human word like war was as foreign to their thoughts as dyslexia is to a normal human. There exist here a logical society of non-angry enhanced humans that cherish their Garden of Eden world in this peaceful sector of space.

I do remember once having a bad dream that the world that I lived on was polluted and corrupt beyond salvage. I try with all of my ability but somehow I can't recall the exact name of that world. I do have vague clue in my mind that it had something to do with the word humans would have used for soil. I can't be sure.

I do suppose that it is merely a vague memory of a bad dream that I had.

I do hope that the wonderful creator that I was extremely sure existed inside of all vibrating atoms everywhere, would never have allowed such a nightmare world called dirt or soil to exist in any of the creator's universes.

Even if time was not a concept to the creator, the reality of Terra Gaia was very beautiful and totally real at all instant moments.

Contently the enhanced Terra Gaia humans now live in each precious moment of current reality. Terra Gaia is a glorious new world of utopia that is indeed perfect for the newness of humankind to always live long and peacefully prosper.

Stories of outside the box thinking are indeed rare among citizens of our present struggling society. It should be possible to easily review someone's extreme possibilities without condemning the imagination of the writer.

It is indeed conceded by this writer, that as vast as all of the universes are, many alternative truths surely do exist elsewhere.

Eric Wilkins
1613 Club Pond Rd.
Henderson N.C. 27537

252-213-5199
spaceman186000mps@gmail.com

ABOUT THE AUTHOR

Full Name,
Donald Eric Wilkins.

But!
I have always gone by Eric Wilkins
my entire life, and I always will.

Born, 1157 pm
December 24, 1950
Henderson N. C.

Loved Astronomy from an early age.

Lived many years on this
Fantastic Spaceship, *Earth*.

My Bucket List is almost complete,
and I will soon go on to
explore the Universe.

The Earth is moving toward Leo at a
dizzying speed of 390 kilometers a second.
That's a little over 242 miles per second.

You're on it too. God speed!

www.ingramcontent.com/pod-product-compliance
Lightning Source LLC
Chambersburg PA
CBHW021327060726
47591CB00006B/1908